Vampire Graduate Scheme

Placement Two:
The Archives

G Clatworthy

ISBN: 978-1-915516-71-8

1 2 3 4 5 6 7 8 9 10

Cover art by Get Covers.

Published by G Clatworthy
www.gemmaclatworthy.com
gemma@gemmaclatworthy.com

Manufactured by IngramSpark
Australia: Ingram Content Group AU Pty Ltd, Melbourne, Victoria.
US: Lightning Source LLC, La Vergne, Tennessee / Allentown, Pennsylvania / Jackson, Tennessee, United States.
UK: Lightning Source UK Ltd, Milton Keynes, United Kingdom. Europe: Lightning Source UK Ltd, with facilities in Germany, France, and Spain.

The authorized representative in the European Economic Area for EU GPSR is Lightning Source France
1 Av. Johannes Gutenberg, 78310 Maurepas, France
compliance@lightningsource.fr
This book was manufactured using paper and ink products in accordance with commercial standards.

Foreword

This book is for anyone who's ever felt like they're working for vampires!

A special thank you to my amazing typo hunters, grammar gurus, and plot pickers who got this story to where it is today. You are awesome!

If you want to support Gemma, you can find her on patreon for exclusive first reads of new stories. You can also join her newsletter for free stories at www.gemmaclatworthy.com and follow Gemma on www.instagram.com/gemmaclatworthy, www.facebook.com/gemmaclatworthy or join the reader's group on facebook: Gemma's book wyrms. And grab a free prequel to the Vampire Graduate Scheme series here: https://books.gemmaclatworthy.com/vampire-graduate-scheme-prequel

Chapter 1

Embrace change. Change is good. It will make you more adaptable and stronger, more able to take on future disruptions.

Elizabeth Bathory – *The First Disrupter*

The tap of my high-heeled shoes on the tiled atrium floor reverberated around the building as I crossed to the lifts. It was the first day back after the New Year's bank holiday and someone had transformed the place, removing the three enormous Christmas trees that had leant an air of magic and whimsy to the sleek headquarters of the Bathory Corporation as if they had never existed.

Now all that decorated the stark atrium were the banners displaying the company's values of Bravery, Overachievement, Loyalty, and Drive under the corporation's logo of a black bat on a red background.

I shivered despite the brightness of the atrium, shoulders

down, chin up, preparing myself for…I didn't know what for. I had no idea what to expect. But everyone I'd told about my new placement had given me a look that was a combination of humour and pity. So, I wasn't expecting anything good.

"Elle!" A familiar voice broke into my anxiety.

"Hi Precious, did you have a nice break?"

"Yeah, it was great to spend time with the family. Did you have any time off?"

I shook my head. Christmas was a time for family closeness and as a foster kid who'd walked out of my last place with a silent vow never to come back, I didn't have a family to spend the holidays with. Instead, I'd worked here. I'd even asked if it was possible to work the bank holidays, but the look my mentor had given me was so full of pity that I'd mumbled that I was just kidding and hurried out of his office.

"Tell me you got some decent presents."

"Er…" I had bought myself a biography of Stephen Hawking to read. "Just some books. You?"

She flipped her braids forward and pointed to a gold ring threaded through one of her plaits. It had a dagger engraved on it. "Mum and Dad got me this ahead of my initiation later this year. I'm going to be a full clan member."

"Cool." I knew nothing about orc clans or traditions, except Precious always carried a large dagger with her for cultural reasons. At least that's what she told the HR Director who had tried to take it away from her during the presentation course we'd attended last year.

"It's later than normal, but I wanted to wait until after university."

"OK."

"You should come! Mum and Dad would love you."

"Ladies!" Tristan's voice boomed unapologetically across the atrium, and he jogged over, his shiny laced shoes squeaking on the tiles. He draped an arm around Precious' shoulders. "What's the happy hap?" he asked without any trace of irony in his public schoolboy posh voice. "How was your break? Did Santa bring you anything good from his bulging sack?"

Precious shoved him off and pulled a face, baring the tusks that protruded above her bottom lip. "You're disgusting."

"Just glad to be back in the old office after Christmas. You ready for the Archives?" He drew out the last word with a timbre that might have been meant to be spooky.

I shrugged. "It'll be fine." I'd told myself that over and over ever since the Christmas party where Elizabeth Bathory herself, CEO of the Bathory Corporation, had told me that was my second placement on the graduate scheme.

"I'm in Risk Management," Tristan said, as if anyone had asked.

"Really?" They had chosen him for Risk Management. "Are you going to build the assessment models?" Keenness shone in my voice, overriding the stab of jealousy in my chest. Using mathematics in the real world would be amazing, something I didn't think I'd get a chance to do in the Archives.

"Not sure. The Director said I could shadow a few teams this week, get a feel for things. But I'll probably end up heading a team in this placement."

Precious guffawed. "You wish. They'll throw you out after a week when they realise you don't understand coding or statistics."

"My art history degree could come in useful. What if I have to risk assess some old paintings?"

"Sounds like your education might be more useful in the Archives. Fancy switching?" It was only half a joke.

"No thanks. Even if risk isn't my thing, I can network better above ground. Catch ya later, losers." He stepped into the elevator and whipped his phone out.

Precious scowled after him. "One day, that grak is going to have an accident…with my fist."

I stifled a laugh. It would do Tristan some good to be taken down a peg or two, but I wasn't entirely sure Precious was joking.

She shook the grimace from her face and replaced it with her usual bright smile. "Have a good day. You'll be great. See you at lunch."

I waved as she followed Tristan into the lift, standing as far away as she could from him. I waited for the next elevator. I was going down, deep into the basement floors where the Archives Department lived. I pressed each finger on my left hand against my thumb in an effort to calm myself with the repetitive motion.

It was fine. It was just another placement. Even if it was awful, it was only a few months then I'd be somewhere new. Unless I messed up again. But how likely was it that I'd uncover another fraud in the Archives? Or that I'd embarrass the company by announcing said fraud at the Christmas party? It wasn't my fault that I hadn't realised the microphone picked up my voice, but no one had been happy. That was why I was punished with this placement. But it would be fine.

I stepped into the elevator.

"Hold the door." The shout cut through my spiralling thoughts, and I pressed the button.

A tall man in a checked shirt and grey trousers with devastating chocolate-coloured eyes hidden behind thick-framed glasses darted into the lift. Liam.

"Going down?" he asked.

I goggled at him. That was too inappropriate, even if we'd shared a dance at the Christmas party. My face reddened. Then I realised he meant the lift. I was so caught up in worrying about my placement that I hadn't selected a floor. I nodded. "Archives."

He gave a low whistle. "Wow, they are testing you, aren't they?"

"What do you mean?" A frown creased my forehead.

"I haven't heard of anyone joining the Archives Department since I've worked here. They must think you're something special."

"Maybe." My frown deepened. I hadn't thought of it like

that. That this placement might be a reward instead of a punishment.

We rode the lift in silence for a long moment before I blurted out, "How was Christmas?" Stupid question. I didn't even know if he celebrated the holiday.

"Lonely. My folks were on a cruise." Some emotion that I couldn't read flickered over his handsome face. "A couple of friends invited me to theirs, but I didn't want to be a third wheel, so I ended up on my own for Christmas and New Year. Sad, right?"

"Totally," I agreed. He looked down at his shoes in embarrassment, so I decided to 'fess up. "I spent it alone too, but I took some work home. So, I guess that makes me sadder?"

"Yeah? Did you order a takeaway too?"

I leaned forward. "Sweet and sour chicken balls."

"Ouch. At least it wasn't turkey."

"You didn't?"

"Yep. With cranberry sauce. And I watched the King's speech."

I winced and put a hand to my heart in mock horror. "Did you end up dressing your pet in a Christmas bow?"

"You have a pet? Then you weren't alone! I win at loneliest Christmas!"

A smile tugged at my lips. "Is that something you want to win at?"

The door opened with a ding, and he stepped out. "See you around, Elle," he said as the doors closed.

I smiled and shook my head. He was weird, but he'd made me forget about my new placement for a couple of minutes and…that dance. It had felt like it meant something, but so much had happened during the party and I'd made sure I was busy at work afterwards, and then there were the enforced bank holidays of the Christmas season…it was easy to push it to the back of my mind. It probably meant nothing, especially since he had a girlfriend. And I had bigger things to worry about than my non-existent love life.

The elevator doors slid open. I had arrived at the Archives.

Chapter 2

There is no magic genie waiting to grant your wishes; you have to make things happen for yourself.

Elizabeth Bathory – *The First Disrupter*

As the elevator doors closed behind me, my first impression of the place was of age. There's a certain smell – part dust, part paper, part leather, part something else – that tells you something has been around for a long time and this basement floor had that scent. The dark wood panelling added to the old aura. It looked original, but the building wasn't old enough to have centuries old panelling in it. At least, I didn't think it was.

I gazed over the polished wooden desk. Behind it was a large wheel with seven display stands for books built into it. One of the display boards had a thick volume on it, held open by a book ribbon that lay across ancient pages.

A corridor stretched away from the desk showing the edges

of shelves that disappeared into darkness. I could make out the first row of shelving, complete with yellowed labels that curled off the wood, but not much more, just the sense that there was a large space back there. When they said Archives, they weren't kidding.

The desk itself was more like an old-fashioned shopkeeper's counter than a tradition desk. It made me nervous, like it was designed to keep the riff-raff out and I was the riff-raff. I'd seen one like it on a school tour of some museum. A stack of papers rested on the desk next to an elaborate inkwell that suggested I had gone back in time to the eighteenth century.

I stepped up to the desk that cut off the shelving from the small reception. The light here was different, muted and reminiscent of candles instead of the electric strip lights that illuminated the upper floors. My feet made no noise on the soft blue carpet.

"Hello?"

No one answered.

Maybe the director was somewhere in the Archives, searching for something. I shifted from foot to foot. Should I venture behind the desk? Precious wouldn't hesitate, but I wasn't as confident as my orc friend. Still, I should probably take some sort of initiative. After all, bravery was one of the company values.

I looked around and found the hinged section that allowed me to cross to the other side. I stood there for a moment, repeating my calming exercise of tapping each finger against my thumb on my right hand. The Bathory Corporation was all about taking the initiative. I lifted the section.

A warm desert wind brushed over my skin, followed by the sticky sensation of cobwebs on my fingertips. Didn't they dust in here? I pulled my hand away and brushed it off.

"Who dares to breach the sanctity of the Archives?" A booming voice echoed around the room.

I whirled around, checking behind me. There was nobody there.

Silver-blue smoke swirled out from the desk.

I dropped the hinged section of the desk and stepped back, gripping my laptop bag. "S-sorry."

The smoke grew into an enormous cloud that flickered with bolts of blue lightning. "Who dares to breach the sanctity of these Archives?"

"Elle, Elle Bruma."

"Elle Elle Bruma, prepare to meet your doom."

The smoke thickened and spread out, engulfing the desk and filling the space in front of me. I backed into the cold metal lift doors and mashed my hand against the panel outside, praying that a lift would arrive.

"Sorry. I was told to come here, but it was a mistake. I'll just leave. Sorry," I babbled, still pressing buttons.

"Who sent you to steal from the Archives?" Golden eyes appeared in the menacing fog, focused on me.

The stench of bad eggs filled my throat and made it hard to

breathe.

"Steal? No! I work here. I have a placement here."

The smoke sucked in on itself and formed a humanoid shape. The voice changed from deep and booming to quizzical. "You have a placement in the Archives?"

I nodded, my mouth too dry to speak.

The humanoid form shrank down until it was a short man, only a couple of inches taller than me. My gaze first caught on his striking gold waistcoat, hung with braiding that fell to his knees. When my eyes had adjusted to the dazzling light that came from the garment, I could focus on his face, which sported a long thin moustache that fell below his chin and the bushiest eyebrows I had ever seen, styled into points that stretched up to his unlined forehead.

His eyes glowed a brighter gold than his waistcoat and, despite his lack of wrinkles, I had the impression that he had lived for a long time. I tore my gaze away and stared at the carpet, catching a glimpse of pointed purple slippers poking out from under baggy black trousers.

He studied me, then shook his head, his short queue of hair shaking in time with his movement. "Nobody tells me anything. Let me see..." He disappeared and reappeared behind the desk where he shuffled through a stack of papers. "Oh, yes. Noelle Bruma. On the graduate scheme. How exciting! I have not had a graduate placement before. But, why did you not ring?"

I looked from his puzzled face to the ornate inkwell that he pointed at. There was a piece of paper next to that said in faded brown letters: *Rub for service.* It was half covered by a stack of papers. I had completely missed it.

"Errr…"

"It is quite simple. If you wanted to speak to me, you should just rub it." I blushed, not knowing where this was going. He took pity on me. "The inkwell. Rub it. That's how I know if someone needs me. Can you follow simple instructions, Miss Bruma?"

"Y-yes."

"Good." He rubbed his hands together. "Good. Yes. Alright, I suppose you can come back here. How *did* you lift the hatch?" He squinted at me, his golden eyes narrowing to slits.

Was that a trick question? I hurried to get behind the wooden desk, shutting the hinged wood behind me. He stood there, waiting for a reply. "I saw the hinges in the wood and lifted it up."

"Hmmmm. I will have to redo the security wards if just anyone can get through. But, at least I can add you to the protocols so you can come and go as you need to. I cannot deal with you waking me up every time you want to go for lunch. Is that something you do?"

"Go for lunch?"

He gave me a look that told me he thought I was stupid. "Eat."

"Yes, I need to eat."

He let out a sigh. "Fine. But no food or drink allowed at all in the Archives proper, Miss Bruma. Do you understand?" He lowered his voice on the final word, making sure that I got the emphasis.

I nodded. "Elle."

"Pardon?"

"Please, call me Elle."

"I see. Informality so soon, this truly is a strange time." He shook his head as if I had let him down. "I am…" he said some syllables that didn't land right in my ears and made my head hurt. "But you may call me Ahmed al-Rhanin, the magnificent, scourge of the Arabian desserts, master of the magical arts, personal server to the Queen of Sheba, adviser to the Kings of Jordan and, latterly, Archivist for the Bathory Corporation. Or, as you prefer informality, you may call me Ahmed, or I will always answer to 'your magnificence'." He gave a low bow, extending one arm with a flourish.

"Pleased to meet you, Ahmed." I bobbed my own bow in return, but refrained from using 'your magnificence', unsure how exactly that title fit into the employee handbook.

"So, what do we keep in the Archives?" I found myself inserting the capital letter. He nodded with a small smile, and I took that as a sign that he appreciated respect for the department.

"Excellent question, Elle. Excellent question."

Chapter 3

The only thing that all labyrinths have in common is that they are always full of surprises.

Georgios Taurus – *A Guide to Labyrinths*

"We provide storage services for anyone who can afford to pay the Bathory Corporation's exorbitant fees," Ahmed said.

"Like a bank vault," I said, keen to show I understood.

He gave a small chuckle and wiped a tear from one of his golden eyes. "Oh no, nothing at all like that. You can break into a bank vault."

I swallowed, put back in my place.

"Here, we provide a secure service. You stand on the brink of the largest magical archive in Britain, outside of Oxford University, but then, they were founded before this corporation, so that is not surprising."

"But what's in there?"

"Aha, the youngling wants to see our secrets. Well, then, Elle of the graduate scheme, come with me and I shall reveal the depths of the Archives." He snapped his fingers and dim lights flickered on above the shelving, dulled by dark green lampshades.

"Is that to protect objects from light damage?"

Ahmed laughed again. "Oh no, that is for the ambience. You cannot be steward of a place such as this and have," he shuddered, "full lighting. I wanted torches of real flame, but the premises team told me that it breached health and safety regulation. Hah! As if half of the items we guard here are not more dangerous than a little fire."

I nodded, not understanding, but not wanting to show my ignorance.

"Do you have any electrical objects on your person? I understand most people now have portable telephonic devices, or so George tells me."

Who was George? I patted my laptop bag and took my phone out of my pocket.

"Leave them here."

He must have sensed my reluctance to part with my technology – I don't think I'd been more than two feet away from my phone since I got it in my early teens, phones not being a priority for foster kids, at least not in the family I was placed with – because he rolled his eyes and opened a drawer.

"They will be perfectly safe here. No one can get past this

desk." He narrowed his eyes at me, "Except apparently our new graduate…but no matter, you can have them back later. And," he added holding up his forefinger, "I shall add an additional layer of protection."

I did as he requested and relinquished my laptop and phone before standing back as he gestured at the drawer. Nothing happened. As pieces of magic went, it was distinctly unimpressive, but maybe that was the point of real magic. Unlike the showy fake stuff that most mundanes enjoyed on TV or in stage shows, this magic was functional and didn't need to prove itself. It wasn't there for entertainment.

Satisfied with whatever spell he'd cast, Ahmed nodded and bowed me into the Archives. "Now, onwards!"

He strode to the shelves. They parted for him, creating an aisle. He continued, oblivious to the display of magic that defied physics and the lights flicking on as he passed in a reverse horror movie pastiche. I scurried after him, not wanting to be left alone behind the desk.

A strange scuffling noise sounded from a long way away.

"What's that?" I whispered, part in awe, part in fear and part because it felt like the right thing to do.

"Oh, that is only the minotaur."

I stopped dead. He had to be joking.

Ahmed turned. "Do not be afraid. They will not harm one who works as a guardian here." He tilted his head to one side. "But, to be sure, do not carry any meat products on your person, they cannot resist the temptation. And perhaps you should not venture here after dark." With that, he continued into the depths of the Archives.

Shelves loomed up on either side of the aisle. Every so often they split off into new avenues, but I couldn't make out a pattern in the spacing. I squinted at the aged labels as we passed. Some were alphabetical, more were unreadable. But the worst were the ones that were clear warnings; cartoon-like illustrations of someone losing their head or dissolving in what might have been acid. I shivered and hurried to catch up with Ahmed.

"How do you categorise everything? Do you use the Dewey decimal system?"

Ahmed stopped and whirled round to face me, one finger raised as he vibrated with anger. "Do not mention that name in my presence. Dewey decimal system, pah." He spat after he said the words. "As if that man," he pronounced the word like a curse, "could create anything complex enough for our storage. I have invented the most ingenious categorisation system in the world, and all anyone knows about is the Dewey – no! Enough about him and his ten-based system. Here, we have more nuance than that man could conceive. Dewey, indeed." Ahmed shook his head, closed his eyes and sucked in a deep breath.

"The Archives," he continued more calmly, "are divided into sections depending on what we house here. It is a complicated business, because many of the objects stored here are magical and do not like to be near other magical items. For example, look here." Ahmed stroked one finger down a wooden box numbered one – five – one. The box edged forward until it protruded enough that he could take it down. "This is The Book of the Dead."

I peered in and saw a book that lived up to its name. Smoky jewels glinted in the blackened leather cover. Was that my imagination, or were the shadows darkening? A low whisper surrounded us.

"It was retrieved from the Temple of Anubis in Upper Egypt during an ill-fated expedition. It is said that any who behold its pages will expire on the spot."

I nodded and gave a nervous smile.

"Open it."

"What?"

"Open the book."

"But you just said–"

Ahmed puffed out his chest and stared down at me. "I am your direct superior, and I gave you an order. Perhaps you are not suited to Archive work. I shall inform Ms Bathory." He shrugged and started to close the box.

"No, wait. Is it safe?"

"What possible reason could I have to want you dead?"

That wasn't an answer. My hands shook, and cold sweat trickled down my spine as I reached for the book. Around me, the shadows cast by the flickering lanterns deepened, sucking the light from the aisle.

I touched the stiff leather binding, my heart pounding as if it wanted to leave my chest. My breaths came in shallow pants.

Ahmed jerked the box away and closed it up with a laugh. "You were actually going to open it. Oh my stars, this is such fun."

"Wait. You didn't want me to open the book?"

"Of course not. It is the Book of the Dead. Any who look upon its pages shall pass into death. I told you that! Besides, that would not be good for our corporation. No, indeed. Why would you want to open it?"

"You told me to!" My voice was loud in the shadowy archives.

"Do not be getting so worked up, Elle. It was a joke. What do you people call it these days? A prank. We have bonded now, yes."

My mouth fell open.

"So serious," he chuckled. "Come." He beckoned me onwards into the ever-shifting gloom of the Archives.

He paused at an unremarkable crossroads in the archives shelving, then turned left. "Here we have rare books."

I leaned forward in the atmospheric light and read the spine of the one nearest to me. "Shakespeare's First Folio. Why do we have it? Shouldn't it be in the British Library or something?"

Ahmed laughed again. "Oh, I am most glad you have joined me for a placement. You are a source of unending amusement.

The British Library houses an edited copy. The original is far too valuable to place under their mundane sources of protection and storage. Here we can ensure that the moisture and lighting levels are perfect and, of course, there are no readers claiming they have a right to it."

"An edited copy?"

"Yes. The original of the Merry Wives of Windsor was much bawdier. It is most indecent. You can read it perhaps. One of the benefits of working here and having access to the knowledge contained in our humble Archives. George likes the rude drawings in our medieval manuscripts."

"Who's George?" I reached out my hand to take another book, the gold lettering on the spine so faded that I couldn't read it where it sat on the shelf. My fingers brushed the leather cover, and I pulled the book from its place. A roar filled the Archives.

Shaking footsteps pounded in an adjacent aisle, hammering closer. I turned in their direction to see a huge creature charging towards me. I froze in horror.

Ahmed flung himself in front of me. "No, no, George. This is Elle Bruma. She is on a placement with us."

The monster stopped and snorted. George took up the entire space between the shelves, his thick torso covered by a skin-tight white shirt that strained to cover his muscles. A skirt made from grey suit fabric clung to his thighs. What I could see of his lower half was covered with thick mottled fur, and his legs ended in enormous black hooves. But the most striking thing about him was his head. George was a minotaur.

His head was that of an angry bull, complete with a delicate gold nose ring and horns that curved away from the side of his forehead before they stretched up, giving him an extra foot of height.

He regarded me with curious brown eyes. "A placement?" His voice was thick, as if he spoke around too many teeth. "Then forgive me, Miss Bruma, I was unaware of this placement." He shot an accusatory glance at Ahmed. "Why did you not tell me? I could have gored her. Do you want to file another health and safety report?"

My hands prickled with sweat, and I leant against the shelves for support. He could have killed me.

Ahmed gave an exaggerated wave of his hand. "I did not know until today. But, now you have met. And there was no incident, so no report. Elle, this is Georgios Taurus. They are our minotaur."

They not he. The thought registered in my mind, along with an embarrassment that I'd assumed they were a 'he' just because they had a hulking body and a bull's head.

"A pleasure to meet you. And please, call me George." They gave a small half bow making the discreet ring in their nose sway.

"P-pleased to meet you, too. What you said about goring me?" I couldn't help myself. I had to know.

"Do not trouble yourself with that. A misunderstanding. Now I have your scent, I know not to attack. Welcome to the

Archives. Do you do hugs?" Without giving me a chance to reply, George pulled me into a warm hug. "So, how long will you be with us?"

"Six months," I mumbled through the hug. Their grassy scent wasn't unpleasant, but it was pungent.

They released me and clapped me on the shoulder. "No time at all. There is much to tell you about the Archives." Someone else who inserted the capital letter. They must love working here. "Ooo, we're going to have fun. I can feel it. Have you shown her the jewellery section?"

"I am working on it. Give me time. We have only just got to books."

"And I bet you were going to maps next. So predictable."

"No." Ahmed rolled his eyes. "I was going to the Atlantis section."

"Next to maps."

Still bickering, they both started moving. I followed behind, hugging my hands tight around my chest. What had I gotten into?

Chapter 4

Many try to memorise a route in and out of a labyrinth, but the truth is that there are only two people who know the layout for certain; the designer and the designated guardian. A minotaur is often selected for this task as the species has an innate understanding of complex mazes. Other methods for intrepid labyrinth explorers include the tried and tested string method and trusting to the gods. One is infinitely more reliable than the other.

Georgios Taurus – *A Guide to Labyrinths*

I tried to keep track of the twists and turns in the labyrinthine Archives, but it was no good. My brain couldn't hold all the information. Ahmed and George walked with confidence and no indication they were lost as they took lefts then rights at what seemed like random intervals, pausing every so often to point out interesting artefacts that we stored here.

The Atlantean section was mostly boring old statues of naked people posing in the way that statues do, but my eyes lit up at a complex series of bronze interlocking cogs stacked on a shelf in between a statue that may have represented 'thought' and another that may have represented 'horny old goat man'.

"What's that?"

"The first computer," said Ahmed dismissively as he moved on.

My eyes went wide. "The first computer," I repeated in respectful awe.

"Oh yes, the Atlantean's were big on technology, but gods were much more active back then. According to legend, the king ordered a giant speakerphone to connect directly with the heavens, but the gods didn't like the idea of being on call all day and night, so Poseidon smote the island nation with a giant wave, washing it under the sea with all their technological advances. Quite the scandal at the time." Ahmed shook his head. "Still, humanity caught up eventually. Not as beautiful as the Atlantean technology but they installed a telephone down here a few years ago, so now anyone in the building can call us." Ahmed sniffed his disapproval.

"Not that they do," George added with a tinge of disappointment.

"Needless to say, as soon as it was installed, I began to sympathise with the gods."

Something about this didn't add up. I had a ton of questions, but I decided to go with the one that made least sense to me.

"You spoke as if you were around at the time of Atlantis…"

It was possible there was a translation glitch. Ahmed spoke English with a rich accent that I couldn't place but reminded me of sand and palm trees and figs, for some reason. But then I also worked for a company owned by vampires, so maybe he really was that old.

"I was. The last king was an arrogant cur who doomed his own people."

I didn't know how to process that, and Ahmed gave me no time to think of a response.

"Take that box down," the Director said.

I swallowed and placed a tentative hand on the small lead box. It was warm to the touch. I offered it to Ahmed, but he shook his head and told me to open it.

"Is this another joke? It won't kill me, will it?"

"Ahmed!" George admonished him. "What was it this time? You can't mess around with mortals, they're not as tough as me. Don't worry, Elle, when I started working here, he tried to get me to drink from Ceridwen's cauldron. It's his idea of a joke. A bad one."

Ahmed chuckled and shook his head. I took that to mean that I wouldn't die if I did as he asked.

The lid rose easily to reveal a smooth black stone with a seam of white crystals sparkling through its centre. It sat in a small depression in the grey silk lining the colour of storm clouds as if it were a precious jewel.

"Take it out," Ahmed ordered. George nodded along behind him, their horns catching one of the green glass lampshades and making the light swing.

I did as I was told, taking the smooth stone in my hand. It was about the size of my palm and had a nice warmth to it. I turned it this way and that but couldn't see anything special about the rock.

"What is it?"

"This is a stone of thunder."

I dropped the smooth stone back into its box like it burned me.

Ahmed chuckled. "Do not worry. They come in pairs. It cannot function without the other, which we store far away. If you were to put them together. Boom!" The last word was accompanied by a rolling crash of thunder.

I hunched my neck into my shoulders and looked around as a sensation of hot wind and desert sands prickled my skin.

Ahmed laughed again. "Do not be afraid. That was me. If I could capture your face now…" He laughed again and transformed.

His face switched. I couldn't think how else to describe it. One minute his moustached face was there, and the next I looked at my own face, pale and shocked, complete with the small blemish between my eye and my ear that I tried to hide with makeup. The only difference was that my head was on Ahmed's body.

He laughed again and switched his face back, slapping his thigh. "Your face!"

"Wha– Wha–?" I couldn't form a full sentence. He had my face. And now he was back. This was the strangest thing I had seen since working at the Bathory Corporation and I'd spent my first placement doing an audit in the fae realm.

Ahmed saw my distress and his face was kind as he took the box from my trembling hands and patted my arm. "I forget that not everyone has seen a djinni."

I stared at the small man. "A genie, like in Aladdin?"

He narrowed his golden eyes at me. "I have seen the film of which you speak. Do I look like a blue comedy figure to you?" To emphasise his point, he turned into an apparition of the animated Disney character. I kept my mouth shut. Now he did look exactly like the blue genie.

He transformed back and grew in stature, filling my vision as he ranted, "One of my brethren decides to consult for an animation company and that film has set up stereotypes for my people that I cannot escape. I am a djinni. A spirit of fire and air with powers that no mere mortal can imagine. Copying your form is but the least I can do."

Clouds swirled around him, building into a cyclone. Wind whipped at the shelves, shaking boxes and books from their careful positions.

"Alright, you made your point," George said, placing one enormous hand on the djinni's shoulder. "We don't want another cataclysmic event down here. Think of the paperwork."

Ahmed stared at George for a long moment, his golden eyes

sparking anger. Then he was himself again, the same small man in odd clothes who had greeted me. The room ceased to shake, and the magical typhoon stopped as abruptly as it had started.

He gave me a small bow. "Forgive me, Elle. It is a burden I have lived with since the nineteen nineties, but it is no excuse for my behaviour. I think I shall take some tea to calm myself. Now, if you will return these to the shelves, I will meet you at the front desk. Our tour is over for this morning." With that, he disappeared. There was no smoke, no warning, he simply was no longer there.

Chapter 5

Of course, I have had failures over the years, but the important thing is to learn from them, and have a strong group of people around you who can help you back to your feet. As I've said before; an individual is nothing without a strong team behind them.

Elizabeth Bathory – *The First Disrupter*

eorge slapped me on the back, winding me as they passed. "You did well. The first time he did that to me, I hid in the labyrinth for a week."

"Er, thanks. So, what should I do with…." I gestured to the dozen boxes and handful of books that now lay on the carpeted floor.

"Put them back, of course."

"Right, sure. But, how do I know where they go?"

"Ahmed!" They snorted. "He thinks that everyone can understand the magical system here without training. You have to use the codes."

"The codes?"

They picked up the box closest to their hooved feet and pointed to a card slotted into a space at one end. "Each item we store here has a code that ties back to our record book. The letters stand for the location. North, South, East, West. Then there's the row – that's this number here. The number after the dash is the shelf, and then this final part tells you its placement on the shelf. So, NW52-1-101 goes….here." It sounded a bit like Dewey's numbering system to me, but I had enough sense to keep that to myself in case Ahmed heard. They placed the box into its place. "It's simple enough, just don't touch anything that has an X at the end."

"Why not?"

George pulled a face. "Those are the magical items potent enough to cause a lot of trouble if not properly handled. We've got one book in here that floods the entire row unless you tickle its spine every time you remove it. But I think we're alright here. No magical items in this row that I can recall, aside from the thunderstone, of course."

"Do you know everything that's stored in this place?"

They huffed out a laugh that was a cross between a snort and a moo. "Not a chance. But I know a lot of the items that need special care. That's part of my duties here in the labyrinth. I'll take you on my rounds tomorrow, if you like." Their face squinted and one of their ears flicked as if they could hear something.

"Thank you, that sounds great." I meant it. It was nice to have someone who wanted to spend time with me and take me under their wing, or hoof, or whatever. My previous placement had been…tense, and made me question whether taking the spot on the graduate scheme was the right thing to do. But maybe here in the Archives of all places, I could find my people.

"I'm just going to check on…" George trailed off.

I picked up a box and squinted as I read the old text. This place could do with some technology. Maybe QR codes or RFID tags to make it easier to find and place these items. My mind turned over the idea. Perhaps I could use my placement to implement a new storage system and leave this place more organised than when I started.

I looked up to mention my idea to George, but they had left.

"Hello?" I called to the empty corridor.

How had someone so large left so quietly? I looked around, hunching my shoulders in the atmospheric and inadequate lighting. I was alone. In a labyrinth.

Panic rose in my chest, clutching at my throat with icy fingers of dread. I leaned back against the shelving and tapped my fingers against my thumbs in a familiar pattern. Seven times on each hand. My lucky number. I pushed myself to take deep breaths, but my lungs worked against me.

Closing my eyes, I chanted algorithms under my breath in time with the second hand ticking round on my ancient Lilo and Stitch watch, taking solace in numbers and forcing my body into rhythmic breathing.

Once I was back in control, I could think. Ahmed and George both knew where I was. They would come back for me. So, all I needed to do was tidy up. Yes. Focus on the task. Interpret the numbers. Place things on shelves, and they would be back for me soon.

With a plan to focus on, I selected a book this time and turned it in my hands to find the code. It was bound in cloth rather than traditional leather and had the smell of age about its curled pages. Curiosity got the better of me so I opened it and read the title printed on the first page: *A Hitchhiker's Guide to the Demon Realm.*

I turned the page and stopped.

There was a picture of someone being tortured. The graphic detail almost leapt from the page. I slammed it shut and closed my eyes. The image was still there in black and white. I had a feeling it would haunt my dreams later tonight.

Shuddering, I found the reference code and placed it back in its place. Two down, only a few more to go.

I placed the others quickly, not daring to open any of the storage boxes that came in every sort of size, colour and material; from red wood to copper green.

In less than half an hour, I had put everything away apart from one book. Pretty good going for my first day.

I was getting used to the codes so put it back in the right spot with ease. As I did so, I noticed one that had been shelved in the wrong place. There was no X on the spine so I took out the slim hardback and held it up to the light to make sure.

The code didn't match the ones around here, it should be somewhere more northerly. I tapped the cover, wondering what to do. I could put it back where I found it, after all, maybe it had been put here on purpose, but the thought of misfiling something deliberately rankled with my neat-loving personality.

I could wait. Ahmed and George were sure to return at some point and I could talk it through with them. But that wasn't a course of action that someone who wanted to be director of her own department by the time she was thirty would do.

I should show some initiative. I was on the grad scheme, after all, that's what people expected of us. I studied the code again. If I followed this aisle, taking care to look at the numbers as I went, I could find out which way was North and find the right place.

Checking to make sure I was still alone and didn't have a better option, I started following the numbers. Nothing could go wrong if I stuck to the code and trusted the maths. It was like making a map, the one part of geography lessons in secondary school that I had enjoyed, checking co-ordinates, plotting the swiftest routes. Much better than doing the actual orienteering that came after the mapwork.

I shuddered at the memory, glad that my current job was inside and warm instead of trekking across the sodden British countryside.

Confident in my approach, I sped up, only checking the

codes every couple of shelves until I came to a crossroads.

Now I had a dilemma, I could continue on the path I was sure would get me there eventually, but I had no idea how large this labyrinth was. I could end up following that corridor for hours. But, I mapped out the route in my mind. If I swung left, I could cut through the next right and I should be further on.

That was how the codes worked. I had to trust them. Maths had never let me down in the past.

A strange gurgling came from straight ahead, echoing down the corridor. That decided me. I'd go left.

I made it about twenty feet before an alarm blared through the labyrinth.

Chapter 6

Of course, the main security system of your standard labyrinth is the complicated series of twists and turns. But, for certain labyrinths, additional security measures are added.

Georgios Taurus – *A Guide to Labyrinths*

I dropped the book and sank to the floor, clutching my ears. The noise cut through my brain, screeching through my synapses and making it difficult to think. I lay frozen on the ground, staring up at the ceiling where the green tinged lights now had a reddish hue that flicked on and off in the universal lighting that signalled an alarm. *What had I done?*

At the far end of the aisle, an orange light crept closer, and I swore a puff of flame flickered. *What was that?* Had I managed to set fire to the place too?

The alarm gave way to pounding footsteps, and Ahmed and

George blinked down at me.

"What are you doing in the restricted section?" Ahmed glowed a dangerous golden red, like liquid fire.

I uncovered my ears, the aftershocks of the siren still ringing through them. Whatever the fire-like light had been, it had gone. I grabbed the book and used the shelves to pull myself upwards, my knees knocking together after the shock. "I wanted to return this."

Ahmed snatched it from me and studied the code. "This is from the other end of the labyrinth. Why do you have it?"

"It was with the books I reshelved." I looked down at the floor and shuffled my feet. This was it. Fired for entering a restricted section of the labyrinth on my first day of the placement. That had to be a record. Not the record I wanted, of course, but I'd at least be remembered. As a total failure.

Hot tears welled up in my eyes.

"Relax, Ahmed, you're scaring her."

"What? Hmmm." With a wave of his hand, the lights turned from red to green.

"I'm really sorry. I d-didn't know it was the restricted section. There wasn't a sign."

George turned sympathetic eyes on me and pointed up to where a large, printed sign swung above our heads. OK, so there was a sign, but it wasn't exactly at my eye level.

"Hmmm," Ahmed clicked his fingers, "we had better reshelve this little mystery, had we not? Come, you can follow me. I have to say, I am impressed that a human figured out the code so quickly. The last work experience fellow we had here was lost for a week before we realised."

My mouth dropped open.

"I am kidding your leg." Ahmed chuckled. "Always so serious. We found him after three days, just before he started eating the books."

I glanced up at George. The minotaur shook their head but said nothing.

Ahmed started walking away. "At least we can confirm the alarms work. You reset them, George, while I return this to its rightful place. We will short cut through this section, yes."

I followed Ahmed along the aisles of the labyrinth. My hands stopped trembling, and I looked around with open curiosity now it seemed like I was keeping my job.

The restricted section contained a lot of boxes hung with heavy chains and elaborate locks. It might have been my imagination, but a faint rattling sounded as if some of the objects tried to escape their bonds.

A large oil painting of a young man with neat hair and a tailored suit watched us as we walked by, his head turning to follow our movements. He gave me a mocking wave as we passed. I shivered and quickened my pace.

The snatches of numbered codes I could see as I hurried to keep up with Ahmed's brisk steps fitted with George's explanation, and I was gratified to see that I was right. Cutting through this corridor and hanging a right got us back on track and soon we were in the right place.

Ahmed let me do the honours, watching with hawkish eyes as I checked the code and put the book back in its assigned place.

"Good," was his only comment before he did an about turn and led us back to the front desk using an entirely different route. Some of the shelves moved as he approached to open new paths, and I wondered if they'd do the same for me.

Back at the reception, Ahmed looked me up and down. "Not too bad, Elle."

"That was a test?"

"Is not everything?"

I didn't know what to say to that, so I looked away from his golden gaze. After a few seconds of interminable silence, I cleared my throat. "So, should I get my laptop and get to work?"

Ahmed nodded with his lips curled up in a smirk.

Oh no, was this going to be another joke? Maybe venomous snakes would spring out from the drawer when I touched it.

My hand shook as I reached for the drawer. My fingers brushed the wood, and there was that same sensation of cobwebs tickling my skin but nothing else. Holding my breath, I gripped the handle and opened the drawer.

Nothing happened. No snakes, no balls of fire, not even an alarm. I was almost disappointed, but then, maybe that was the point of this test.

I took my laptop bag out and slipped my phone back into my pocket, fighting the urge to sigh with relief. I hadn't realised I was so dependant on my smartphone and how strange it had felt to be without it, even for a short amount of time. That was something to chat through with the Bathory Corporation counselling service, if I ever got round to phoning them again.

Adding calling the counselling hotline to my mental to do list, I unzipped my bag and retrieved my laptop, which I flipped open. "Can I work here in reception or is there somewhere else I should go?"

When I didn't get an immediate answer, I twisted my neck and froze. Ahmed had a considered expression on his smooth, ageless face. I shifted under his scrutiny. It was disconcerting to be looked at like I was a problem to be solved. Was that how I looked when I studied my accounting textbooks?

"Is everything alright?" I asked.

Ahmed's brow crinkled before clearing. "Hmm? Oh, yes, tickety tockety. I must have made an error with the warding spell on the drawer."

I blanched. "You mean my laptop was left unsecure?"

Ahmed laughed. "Hardly not secure. We are in the Bathory headquarters, and there are powerful wards around my desk. One little drawer would hardly matter. No, no."

I nodded, still uncertain. He was the boss, after all, but I didn't fancy having to explain to IT that my laptop had gone missing, even if it was password protected and encrypted.

I set up my laptop on the polished wooden desk and answered a few emails. When I checked the time, I was surprised to find that it was already half past twelve and, yes, there was the email from Precious saying she was going to lunch. About ten minutes ago. Drat. I was late.

"Must you be so loud with the clicking and the clacking? It is giving me quite the headache."

"Sorry. I'll try to type quieter."

Ahmed nodded and poked my silver laptop with his finger. "I never understand the need to get so much information and power in such a small place."

I didn't want to get fired on the first day of the placement, especially not after the misstep in the restricted section, so I bit the inside of my cheek to refrain from mentioning anything about powerful djinn dwelling in an inkwell.

I tapped off another email instead and Ahmed sighed. "Enough already. Enough. I need a break from this."

I paused. "So, what should I do, now?"

"You need regular sustenance, yes? You are human?"

I nodded. I was a regular human, even if growing up I had longed for supernatural powers, I'd never had so much of a flicker of anything supernatural about me.

"Then go, eat." He waved me away.

As I entered the lift, I saw a golden cloud getting sucked into the inkwell.

Chapter 7

Relaxation is not something I typically indulge in, but restoration is important. I find that a healthy diet, exercise and good conversation is often all that is needed to restore the balance.

Elizabeth Bathory – The First Disrupter

I made my way to the staff canteen for lunch, where Precious and Tristan already sat at a table with a couple of the other graduates. The smell of hot food drifted over the large room set out with rectangular tables on a tiled floor. My mouth watered at the scent of chips and some sort of tomato pasta that was the day's special.

I sat down and took my lunchbox out of my bag. The pang of inadequacy I felt in situations like this twanged in my belly. I might be on a well-paid grad scheme, and the organic food in the canteen might be subsidised, but London rents were ridiculous, and I had to budget. I eyed Tristan's large portion of fish and hand-cut chips. Some of us didn't have a rich daddy paying our way. Some of us didn't even know who our parents were.

Not that I felt sorry for myself, just sometimes it would be nice to feel grounded, like I belonged somewhere. I had hoped that getting my dream job would ease that longing with a work family, but given how my day had gone so far, that seemed further away than ever.

No matter. I just had to work harder, be better and work out how to impress my new boss.

"That sausage is pathetic," Tristan sneered, jabbing his fork at Precious' plate.

"I can't help it if you're jealous that mine is bigger than yours."

Tristan frowned down at his plate. "I don't have a sausage."

Precious grinned, showing her orc tusks. "You heard it here first."

The rest of the table exploded into titters of laughter that drew attention from the more senior employees. A couple of managers who I knew were vampires licked their lips.

Tristan reddened and pushed back his mop of brown hair. I covered a snort and had a bite of my cheese sandwich. The bread was stale, but the cheese was sharp, and I'd layered in the overripe tomatoes my flatmate insisted on buying because they were healthy, but always failed to eat. Waste not, want not.

"Go on, have a chip," Precious offered, pushing her plate in my direction. She'd opted for a halfway house; a homemade sausage sandwich with a portion of canteen chips. Maybe my budget could stretch that far, at least once a week. I selected a chip – not too big, I didn't want to take the mickey – and savoured it, allowing the salted hot potato goodness to linger on my palate. "The sign said they were healthy so the vamps don't eat too many saturated fats when they suck our blood." She still hadn't got over the company policy that let vampires use junior employees as juice boxes.

"We were saying we ought to have a night out," Tristan said, trying to brush over the teasing about his sausage.

"You said it." Precious corrected him before taking a large bite of her sandwich.

"Details." Tristan waved away the interruption. "This Friday, after work."

"Maybe," I said.

"See, she's not a spoilsport." Tristan stuffed three chips into his mouth and leaned back in a self-satisfied way.

Precious ignored him. "How's the Archives?"

"Something else," I said. "There's ancient stuff down there."

"I heard they have a dragon," Mandy, a quiet graduate, leaned forward.

I thought back to the burst of fire I had glimpsed when I'd triggered the alarms. A dragon? I was lucky to be alive. I swallowed. "I haven't seen it. The place is huge though." I frowned as I tried to puzzle out the size. It was larger than the ground floor surface area of this building, so how did that work? The Bathory Corporation didn't lease the surrounding buildings, did they? Unless they sublet the basements. Was that a thing?

"So what sort of stuff have they got down there?"

"Books, mostly and boxes." Everyone looked unimpressed. "I saw a couple of statues too."

The conversation moved on when they realised that as mysterious as the Archives' reputation was, I was a useless source of information.

"Well, I've spent the day shadowing credit underwriters. You wouldn't believe the sort of things people have on their bank statements." Tristan leaned in and lowered his voice. "One chap had a payment to his other half for BJ money." He laughed.

Precious choked on her sausage. The spluttering and giggling from our table caused the vampires to move in. I stiffened as they approached us like sharks.

Graduates were open prey for any more senior employees. The only protection we had were the yellow plasters the vampires handed out after they'd fed and the lanyards that hung from our necks. We had to turn them to their bright yellow side once someone had fed on us so we didn't get too depleted – we still had to work, after all.

I fingered my badge with one hand while my other went through the reflexive tapping exercises I used to calm myself. I don't think I'd ever used them this much in one day before.

A female vampire ran her finger down Tristan's neck. He stopped moving, his eyes wide with fear and his nostrils flaring.

"You'll do nicely," said the vampire before sinking her teeth into his neck. After a few seconds, she lifted her head, licked the wounds to close them, handed Tristan a yellow plaster, and walked off with a sway of her hips.

"No fair, Nissy, I wanted that one." The dark-skinned male vampire pouted after her as he sized up the rest of us. His gaze lingered on Precious. She bared her teeth at him. He smirked and came to stand behind me instead.

I tilted my head to one side to get my long ponytail out of the way. It wouldn't do to annoy a senior manager.

"Takes all the fun out of it, but alright," the vampire said. Then he bit me.

I couldn't stop the gasp that left my mouth. There was a moment of stabbing pain before the chemicals in vampire saliva took over and numbed the sensation.

The vampire lifted his head. "Ugh, you taste awful. Are you on medication?" He spat onto his fingers and rubbed them over the holes on my neck before handing me a yellow plaster to show that someone had already fed off me.

I shook my head as I turned my badge to the yellow side as an extra deterrent to anyone else who might want to feed on me. The company policy stated that junior employees couldn't be drained more than once a week, so I was safe for a few days.

Still grumbling about my foul taste, the vampire grabbed

Mandy who'd stood to empty their tray into the bin and clamped his teeth into her neck.

She screamed in surprise and dropped the tray with a clatter on the tiled floor. All heads swivelled to her.

The vampire released them. "Much better." He grinned and sauntered off.

Mandy sank to the floor, scooping up her rubbish and the tray with a fearful glance around the room. That was my worst nightmare; to be the centre of attention. Just being in close proximity to her embarrassment brought cold sweat to my back.

I pushed my chair back and offered to help. She smiled gratefully and I helped her collect the cutlery and a crisp packet from the floor.

The diners stopped watching the display and went back to their meals or, in the case of the vampires, nursing their drinks of choice.

Vampires subsisted on blood, but they could eat small amounts of regular food if they chose to. Most did not. Some ventured into teas and coffees, but I knew the canteen served warm blood on tap for those who wanted it. Free blood packets were one of the vampire perks of working at the Bathory Corporation, right after being able to feast on the junior employees.

"Thanks," said Mandy as she dumped her tray onto the rack set up near the bins.

I nodded. "No problem."

"I think that's the first nice thing anyone's done since I've been here."

"Nice doesn't get things done." I shrugged. This company was cut-throat, but the rewards in the long term would be worth it.

Mandy glanced around and lowered her voice. "God, I hate it here. You'd think the money would be enough, but it's not. Not for this." She jerked her head and pressed her hand to the fresh red bite mark on her neck.

I didn't know what to say. "It'll get better."

"Do you think so?" Hostility rang through her words.

But I had to believe it would.

She gave me a pitiful look and scurried off to clear her tray and escape the canteen.

I finished my sandwich quickly, not registering the taste. Around me, my fellow graduates were doing the same.

Only Tristan attempted to lighten the mood. "I've had worse hickies in nightclubs in Soho."

"You wouldn't last two minutes there after dark." Precious raised her eyebrows at him in a clear challenge.

"Have too."

"Have not."

I left them to their bickering, closed my lunchbox and headed back to the lifts. As I was leaving the canteen, I heard someone call my name.

My heart sank as I looked round and saw Kylie – my assigned graduate buddy – click clacking her way towards me on skyscraper heels.

Chapter 8

Appearance is everything.

Elizabeth Bathory – *The First Disrupter*

"Hi Kylie. What do you want?" I said with a sigh. She had not been kind to me in my first placement, and I doubted she wanted to kindle a friendship now.

"No need to be like that. I'm your buddy, after all." She tried for a smile. It made her look like a skull. Kylie's collarbones stuck out, visible through her fitted shirt and her wrists were like sticks. Her cheeks had a sunken look to them that added shadows to her face.

"Are you alright?" Genuine concern welled up in my breast. She could have cancer or some horrible wasting disease. I could at least be polite.

"Of course I'm alright, you dimwit," she snapped. "I'm being nice." Kylie spat out the word and adjusted her high-end High Street suit.

Any sympathy I had dissipated. "What do you want?"

"I told you. I'm checking in." She gave me a playful punch on the arm. There was no power to it, it was like being hit by a puppy. "Seeing how my buddy is doing." She gave me another grin that stretched her mouth and made her look like a cadaver. It was, in a word, unsettling.

My face said I didn't believe her.

She sighed and crossed her arms. "Fine. If you must know, I've had some feedback that I need to brush up on my personal skills."

I kept my face straight.

"And, even though I'm a delight, apparently I need other people to think that. It's bloody hard here, you know. You have to be strong and tough and 'don't show your emotions' because then I get all the 'little woman' comments and asked if I'm on my period. But now I need to have empathy and be nice too if I've got a shot at a permanent role."

"That sounds like a lot." I channelled my best impression of my agony aunt flatmate.

"It is." Kyle sagged for a moment before she recovered her perfect, confident posture. "Anyway, if anyone asks, could you tell them I've checked in? That I take an interest in your wellbeing?"

"Do you?"

"Sure, you're in audit, right? How's it going?"

"My placement is in the Archives."

She burst out laughing. "Bloody hell! Yes, that's right. Well, they had to punish you somehow after the disaster at the Christmas do. How is it?" Kylie leaned forward, the potential for my misery making her interest genuine.

"It's alright." I shrugged. She didn't need to know about my first day.

"All dusty books and boxes?"

"There's some interesting artefacts." I felt I needed to defend my new department. "I saw a genuine thunderstone." Never mind that I hadn't known what a thunderstone was before this morning.

"Well as long as you're finding it interesting." She put an emphasis on 'you're' as if my idea of interesting didn't match up to hers. Maybe she was right. I didn't know anyone else who enjoyed coding chess games or reading maths textbooks for fun. "So, do you need anything?" Kylie studied her pointed nails.

Did I need anything? I wanted support and reassurance that I was doing alright. I wouldn't get that from Kylie. I needed to impress my boss if I wanted any praise here. "How did you impress the management team in your placements?"

Kylie snorted. "You and I are totally different. I am competent and know what I want. You seem to bumble through your work, so what works for me won't work for you." She looked me up and down, a sneer curling her red lips. "Find a problem and solve it. And if you can't do that…suck up."

"Thanks." I couldn't keep the sarcasm out of my voice, but Kylie didn't notice.

"Glad to help. Remember to tell anyone who asks that I was supportive." With that, she turned her back to me and strutted across the atrium floor, her heels clacking on the tiled floor. Three paces away, she stopped and spun on her heels. "I'm running a focus group on Friday."

"That's nice."

"You moron. I want you to be there. I'll email the details." With that, she headed off.

That was the nicest she'd ever been to me since we'd been assigned as buddies; she must be under pressure if she was willing to have a civil conversation with someone she had made clear was so far beneath her notice.

This company brought out the worst in a lot of people. But it was the best place to work in the city and it gave me the status, if not the belonging, I craved. Not to mention the independence it could give me once I was in a position to make real change. I sighed as I allowed myself to daydream. This was all I wanted.

A frown puckered my face. What sort of focus group was Kylie running?

My phone rang, pulling me out of my introspection as I saw an unknown number flash up. "Hello?"

"Elle, good, you answered. I was not sure the telephone would connect with an outside number."

"Ahmed?"

"Who else would it be? There is a box at reception. Please be so kind as to bring it down when you return from your midday repast."

"I'm on my way now." This was a chance to impress him and prove I wasn't a total incompetent buffoon.

Chapter 9

Before new artefacts are entered into the Archives, they are assessed for magical properties and assigned a catalogue number. If known, their provenance should also be recorded.

Bathory Corporation Guide to Archiving, vol 2

I hurried over to reception and asked for the box for the Archives. The handsome receptionist – I'd noticed that the majority of employees at Bathory Corporation looked like they could model in their spare time, if they had any – checked me on their systems, raised a shaped eyebrow when he realised I did indeed work in the Archives, and handed me the box.

It was a large cardboard box that looked unimpressive but was awkward to carry even though it didn't weigh that much. I asked the receptionist if he knew what was inside, and he gave me a pitiful look as he told me it wasn't his job to open the post.

Put in my place, I hurried back to the Archives.

As I stepped into the lift, my high heel caught on something and I fell forward. I twisted to protect the box. I couldn't mess up a simple delivery.

Just before I hit the floor, strong arms caught me, and I looked up into Liam's chocolate-brown eyes made larger by the lenses in his thick-framed glasses.

"Have a nice trip?" he smiled down at me.

I made a gargling noise.

"It's only a joke." He pulled me upright, his slight frown making the bags under his eyes seem larger. Had something happened? I hadn't noticed those this morning, not that I was paying close attention to his face. Not at all. "Didn't you see the signs?"

I looked around, and there were indeed several yellow warning triangles set up with a picture of a stick figure tripping over a hazard. I lifted the box. "It's hard to see over this thing. What are you doing? I thought you worked in IT?"

"I do. Most of the time it's helping ancient vampires turn on their laptops, but occasionally they let us out of the basement to set up the cables for the conference suite."

"Lucky you."

"I know, right." He nodded solemnly. "What about you?"

I lifted the box half an inch again. "Taking deliveries for the Archives. It's a glamourous job, but someone's got to do it."

We both smiled at each other, the sort of shy smiles that said we were friends but maybe there was something more beneath that.

Then his boss ruined it by shouting over to Liam. "Stop flirting and get that extension cable sorted. Do I need to come over there?"

"No," he shouted back. There was an edge of panic in his voice. I understood. I didn't want to let my boss down either.

"I'd better go," Liam said. "See you around." He pressed the lift call button for me and moved a yellow sign out of my way so I could get in.

"Thanks," I said, unable to think of anything better as the doors closed and I made my way back to the Archives.

Ahmed was waiting for me behind his desk. "You got it."

I lifted the box to indicate that I had indeed got it.

"Good, good. This will be an excellent introduction to the Archives filing process. Bring it here."

I walked through the hinged section of the desk that he held open for me and placed the box on the polished countertop where he indicated.

"Now, we never know what might be sent to us, so it is always prudent to be prepared."

"What sort of things do you get sent normally?"

Ahmed shrugged. "Old manuscripts, precious heirlooms, and once, we got a skull from a cannibal chief."

I laughed, thinking he was joking, but Ahmed's expression didn't change. Not joking then.

"The first thing we do is check for magic. You should stand back. Sometimes there are protective spells or curses that lash out. That is how I lost my first assistant. Foolish wizard. He should have known better." Ahmed shook his head.

I waited for the punchline, but Ahmed's ageless face had become introspective with his gaze fixed on a darker spot on the desk. *Was that a scorch mark?* I squinted at it.

"So, let us get the on with it." Ahmed muttered a number of incantations in ancient languages at the box.

I shrank back.

The cardboard box stayed where it was.

"Alright." Ahmed rubbed his hands together. "Now we have established there are no curses on the box – make a note of that – let us open her up."

I opened up my laptop and tapped some notes. No doubt there was a system I would have to upload these onto later. "Do I need to record which spells you used?"

Ahmed waved his hand at me. "Standard curse detection."

I noted that down.

"Are there usually curses on items you store?"

"More than you might be thinking. But then, not all of the artefacts we have here were obtained legally." He must have caught the look on my face, because he carried on. "It is not our job to judge, it is our job to store. Where provenance is in doubt, we can report to the authorities."

"It doesn't sound safe."

"If you want to be safe, try auditing, not guarding the Archives." Ahmed softened his voice, which had become booming and unearthly in his defence of his department. He clearly hadn't ever audited the fae realm, because my last placement had been anything but safe what with the murderous sea creatures and criminal director. "Besides, do not be worrying about curses. Cardboard is a dampener for some magics, that is why it is so useful for storage and it keeps the posties safe. We have one of the original prototypes for the cardboard box somewhere. Gair experimented with shapes for quite some time before determining the dull sides of a standard box were the best option. The pyramid option was inspired, but the triangular tendencies to enhance magic offset the dampening effect he wanted."

I wondered how someone had found out that cardboard was a dampener and how many cursed items went through our postal system every day. Ahmed interrupted my mental calculations with a shwing of metal.

The djinni took out a long letter opener in the shape of a curved sword from somewhere in the desk and slit the tape holding the box shut. Using the tip of the blade, he lifted the flaps slowly, millimetre by millimetre.

Something like a sigh came from inside. "Interesting," he said.

I typed, providing a modern soundtrack to something that felt like it should have been an ancient ritual.

Ahmed said a few more mystical words, then, satisfied that

the contents had no additional curses on them, he lifted out a small wooden box. "Gabon ebony, if I am not mistaken with unicorn ivory inlay. Powerfully protective. Ah, here's a note." He picked up a piece of paper while my fingers raced over the keyboard to keep up with his assessment of the box.

I paused over 'unicorn ivory' and questioned Ahmed.

"Very rare. Counters magic. My guess is whatever lays inside is a powerful object. Either that or it is from a rich family." He shrugged and turned back to the note, which looked like it was handwritten in ink.

"A riddle, of course." Ahmed shook his head, sending his queue of hair from side to side. He tossed the piece of paper to one side. "It's a fae artefact."

I picked it up. " 'Heart of fire, cold as snow. Touch if you dare.' What does it mean? And shouldn't it rhyme?" Didn't all riddles rhyme?

Ahmed shrugged. "It is probably translated from ancient Fae and words that rhyme do not always translate to English. For example," he said some words in another language that sounded like a rock gargling. "See, beautiful but in English it translates as rubbish. Besides, this is from the fae, who knows what they are thinking? It could be meaningful; it could be nonsense. You never know with the fae. Now let's get this box opened up."

As he lifted the lid, a whoompf sound came from the small box. I ducked on instinct. The fireball surged out of the box and left a rosette on the ceiling.

Chapter 10

Do not open a box of unknown provenance without first erecting a shield.

Bathory Corporation Guide to Archiving, vol 2

Ahmed flapped at his burning moustache. The smell of scorching hair curled around us. I snatched up a glass of water from the desk and threw it in his face.

He stopped moving and levelled a disapproving look at me. His long moustache strands hung dripping from his upper lip, offsetting his hard look somewhat. "I am a being of fire and sand; I do not need water to put out a piffling fire."

I clamped my lips shut so I didn't ask him why a being of fire and sand had been waving his hands at his moustache instead of controlling the flame.

He made a motion with his hand and a surge of heat flowed through the reception area, drying off his moustache which settled back into its usual sleek grooming.

Ahmed glared at me as I made a note of the fireball. I stopped typing.

"Excellent. You got my package." A deep voice sounded over the lobby and I looked up to see the fae emperor standing just outside the lift, looking up at the scorch marks above our heads.

"Emperor Llyr, welcome to the Bathory Corporation. I didn't hear the lift…" Ahmed had a hint of accusation in his voice, and I noticed he didn't bow. Maybe having a 'magnificent' in your title outranked a mere emperor.

The emperor smiled, but no warmth spread through his face. "One of your employees owes me a favour. I had her portal me in."

Ahmed frowned. Portal travel within the company was strictly controlled. I only knew of one fae who did it for the corporation, but perhaps all fae could create portals.

"I shall have to inform our internal affairs team. Is their debt to you paid?"

"That is between me and the debtor, as you well know, djinni." Now the emperor's voice held an undercurrent of warning.

The two supernaturals stared at each other for a while before the emperor smiled again, with all the warmth of a glacier. "So, did you like my item?"

Ahmed raised a styled eyebrow. "We were on the brink of opening it."

The emperor gestured for the djinni to go ahead and watched with an amused expression on face. Like the first time we'd met, I thought his thin and angular face with his pointed teeth made him look like a predator choosing his time to pounce.

This time, Ahmed conjured a shimmering shield in front of us before he eked the box open with exaggerated slowness.

Another puff of fire shot out. Prepared, Ahmed dismissed it with a wave of his hand to reveal the contents of the box.

Ahmed let out a low whistle. "Is this the Crown of Winter?"

The emperor nodded.

I leaned forward and saw a circlet of bare branches covered with frost. A few blood-red berries peeked out from between the boughs. It didn't look like much of a crown.

"May I?" Ahmed asked, his hands poised over the crown.

The emperor nodded again.

Ahmed reached for the crown, paused, and muttered some words.

The emperor's small smile faded. "You found the darts."

Ahmed wagged his finger at the fae. "Hogweed and purple nightshade. Naughty."

The emperor shrugged.

Ahmed lifted the crown, and frost began to spread down his fingers. The djinni shivered, tilted it back and forth in a quick assessment before dropping it back into its case.

"Only fae from the Court of Winter may touch it without harm," the emperor said as he walked forward. He leaned over the counter and shut the box with a click. "Shall I reset the magic?"

Ahmed inclined his head. "May I ask why you have it and not the," Ahmed paused and looked like he was doing some complicated maths, "Queen of Winter?"

"Queen Ilexa asked me to look after it for a while. The fallout from Skathi's ill-judged fraud has been far reaching." The emperor sighed. "I never expected to miss that backstabbing worm, but at least I could rely on Skathi to scheme in an expected manner. His brother is another matter, and he is preparing a claim to the Winter Court as well as his own domain. But that is not your concern. Can you keep the crown safe?"

Ahmed's mouth twitched, and he placed a hand over his heart. "I am offended that you would ask. The Archives are unbreachable."

"Good." The emperor tapped his index finger on the desk. "And forgive me for asking, but, the protocols must be observed."

Ahmed nodded. "For an artefact such as this, we will make sure it is in the restricted section and protected by our most powerful protective spells and…other measures."

The emperor leaned back. "Good. And now, to the matter of price. I don't suppose you would accept payment in our currency?"

Ahmed raised an eyebrow. "The Bathory Corporation does not accept maple syrup, but we will allow fae gold."

"Of course." The emperor reached a hand into his pocket and pulled out a large bag made of soft leather that glistened in the soft light of the Archives. "I trust this will be sufficient for six months of storage."

Ahmed took the bag and emptied it onto the desk with the rich clunk of heavy coins. I stared. It was more money than I could dream of. I didn't know Fae Gold to British Pound exchange rates, but if that was pure gold, I could buy my own London house with the sum that sat gleaming on the desk. Even one coin would be worth more than my entire savings account, although given the paltry amount that sat in there, that wasn't the best analogy.

Aware I was staring and hadn't made any notes for a while, I tapped the name of the artefact and the payment agreed in gold onto my laptop. "How much is it?" I asked, my gaze pulled back to the shining pile of coins.

The emperor raised one shoulder as if to say that trivial details like amounts of money didn't bother him, but his gaze bore into me, his eyes like twin shards of flint.

Ahmed conjured a set of brass scales, weighed the coins and read out a number that I jotted down. "About three hundred thousand pounds," he said, as if that was a normal amount to hand over. "We'll have to take this to the vault."

I wrote that down as well.

The emperor regarded me for a long while before he spoke. "You are the employee who uncovered the fraud with Skathi."

I nodded.

"Have you given any thought to your favour?"

I shook my head, struck dumb by the powerful fae's attention. He had offered me a favour in return for my part in revealing Skathi's fraud last year, but I was trying to put my audit placement behind me. What were the limits of his power? Could I ask him to erase my student debts? Or get me a promotion to Director of my own department? No. I shook the thought away. I would earn my place here.

The emperor took my silence as the denial it was and flashed his teeth at me. "Let me know when you decide." With a sweep of his long coat, he turned and strode through a portal that appeared behind him at just the right moment for his exit to look nonchalant and impressive.

I breathed out a sigh of relief that he had gone. Having that much focus levelled at me was unnerving and not something I was used to. I glanced at the gold again and then met Ahmed's gaze.

He stared at me in a mixture of wonderment and awe, as if I were a mythical beast. Although, as he probably dealt with mythical beasts daily, maybe it was more accurate to say that he looked at me as if I were a new piece of technology he had to deal with but couldn't understand.

"*You* are in possession of a favour from the fae emperor?"

Chapter 11

Nothing ever stays the same for long in a labyrinth.

Georgios Taurus – *A Guide to Labyrinths*

The following day, I arrived at work keen and ready to learn. George had promised to take me on their rounds, and I wanted to know more about the labyrinth; how it worked, what was stored there and, most importantly, how to find my way out.

I had some time to kill before George arrived, so I checked my emails and found one from Kylie informing me that her workshop had moved to next week. There was a group mail to all graduates reminding us about a course we had to attend as part of the programme and a company-wide missive telling everyone not to engage with protestors outside the head office and to call security if things got too heated.

This early in the morning, I hadn't seen anyone camped outside the building, but I had encountered one of them a few months ago; a fanatic who hated supernaturals and blamed vampires for all the ills in the world – a scary combination of deluded and dedicated. A deep shame swept through me that I belonged to the same race as these radicals, and I resolved to be better even if my fellow humans weren't.

The stamp of George's hooved feet approached from inside the labyrinth. *Did they sleep here?*

"Elle!" They pulled me into a hug.

I tensed, unused to this much affection from a co-worker, but it wasn't unpleasant apart from…I screwed up my face. "What is that smell?"

George released me and gave me a sheepish – or should that be cowish? – look. "That would be the fish." They offered me a backpack that did indeed reek of fish, vinegar and fire.

"What is that?" I tried not to gag.

"It's some of what I need for my rounds. I thought you'd want to get involved." They had a matching, if a lot larger, bag on their own broad shoulders.

I took the backpack and nodded, eager to show that I wanted to learn everything about the Archives, even the parts that stank. If I breathed through my mouth, it was fine. Sort of.

I shut my laptop in the drawer Ahmed had shown me, deciding that the risk of theft was minimal, but I took my leatherbound notebook in case I needed to jot anything down. I loved notebooks and so far had matched a new notebook to each placement. For the Archives, I'd chosen one bound in simple red leather with a brass clasp that reminded me of books I'd seen in a library at a stately home I'd visited on a school trip.

"Should we tell Ahmed?" I asked, glancing at his inkwell.

George shot the well a fond look. "No point, he's not an early riser. I think yesterday was the first time I'd seen him out of his bottle before midday since the incident with the dragon."

"Dragon?"

"Not to worry, that was decades ago. Come on." George strode into the labyrinth, paused and handed me a large ball of twine. "You won't need this if you're with me, but sometimes the old methods are the best. If you come in on your own, use the string."

They carried on, and I trotted behind, trying to count the turns they made. "I wouldn't bother," they shot over their shoulder as they spotted what I was doing.

"Why not?"

"The labyrinth changes all the time, it's part of the enchantments."

"How do you find your way?" I wrinkled my brow as a section of shelving in front of us swung forward to block our path, forcing us to take a right-hand turn. And how did the string work if the labyrinth changed?

George didn't break their brisk pace. "I'm a minotaur. We're built for labyrinths. I can't explain it, but I always know where I'm going in here, how to get there and how to get out."

That was clear as mud.

"Don't worry so much. The labyrinth picks up on emotions. It makes it harder for people who aren't used to it. That's one of the enchantments. But it'll get used to you once you've been here a while. Here's our first stop."

A low chittering sounded from near the top of the shelves, like cicadas but with a language behind it.

George gestured for me to open my backpack. "Get the chips out."

I dug around and found a package of greaseproof paper that smelled of strong vinegar. They nodded and retrieved a bowl from among the shelves. The clicking sound increased in volume.

I emptied the chips into the bowl, and George put it on the floor. As soon as the bowl touched the paved path, a swarm of bugs descended from near the ceiling.

I shrieked and swatted at the palm-sized things flapping around my face. George grabbed my arm and pulled me back, out of the direct path of the swarm. They shone a torch at the bugs to reveal cobalt blue humanoid creatures with translucent wings diving to pick up chips that were half their size.

"Cornish piskies. They're tricky things, but they're mostly interested in anyone with food. They can smell carbs from half a mile away, and anyone venturing into the Archives who isn't employed here will take food with them just in case they get lost. We've got a deal with the piskie queen to keep some of them here. They seem to enjoy it, although sometimes they rearrange the shelves. They don't venture too far though, and their filing system is rudimentary; they always move everything from the bottom to the top and then back again. We've filled this section with decoy boxes, so it doesn't mess with the system."

I looked around and saw that none of the boxes were marked with the careful codes that delineated the actual artefacts stored in the Archives.

"Right, onwards." George marched through the swarm, which had thinned now the plate of chips had dwindled down to the last few.

I stepped over a pair fighting over one of the remaining chips and hurried to catch up with George's long strides.

We continued in silence, with George stopping every now and then at random intervals to check the wards and other protective spells were in place. After the third one, I started to recognise the symbols carved into the shelves that denoted the placement of spells, although I couldn't see or feel anything different, except a light dusting on my skin as I passed through some of the magical barriers. George didn't comment, so maybe that was normal. It wasn't like I'd grown up surrounded by magicals, and, like most humans, I didn't know how it worked.

Ignorance was the fuel that lit the hatred of those protesting the largest openly supernatural owned company in the UK, and I resolved to pay attention and learn more.

"Want to see something funny?" George asked.

"Always."

They pulled down a large manuscript that had the whiff of age to it and started turning the pages with their thick fingers. "Here," they chuckled and handed me the book. "These always make me giggle."

They pointed at an illustration of a man in the boat that made up the letter E.

"Is that guy naked in a boat?" I blinked. The man's back formed the back of the E and he had a long flag streaming out from the top of his head forming the top bar with the boat made up the bottom of the letter. His arms held out in front of him made the centre line of the capital E.

George snorted. "Yeah, and look at him holding the duck." There was indeed a colourful duck drawn mid-flight in the man's hands making up the midway line in the E. "What do you think the person who commissioned it asked for?"

"Er, naked duck-powered sailing?"

George doubled over and slapped their thigh, letting out another large snort. "Exactly." They wiped away a tear. "Oh, we're going to have some fun."

After that, George showed me three more illustrations as we made our rounds, including a guy in a dress bending over while someone else watched, rabbits jousting on snails and a man pissing in a pot while holding a large bunch of flowers that made up a K.

Every so often, George would find something out of place

and reposition it somewhere else. I tried to keep track so I could help in the future, making notes in my book as we walked.

"I think you'll like this," George said, coming to a halt in front of a large arched doorway carved in stone. Where a door should have been, a faint blue barrier shimmered like water. They stepped through, ducking their head to get through the arch without scraping their horns on the stone.

I followed, and the cool sensation of water hit my face. Great. This was my best suit, and it was dry-clean only. I hurried forward.

The curtain of water hadn't soaked me through, but it had coated me with a fine sprinkling of water droplets, like walking through a thick mist. I brushed off what I could before looking around. My mouth fell open.

After the atmospheric darkness of the labyrinth, the brighter light in the cave made everything stand out in sharper relief.

We stood in an underground cavern that stretched as far as my eyes could see. Above us, long strands of moist green plants trailed from the roof of the cave, hanging in thick green clumps next to dripping stalactites. Under our feet, thick moss cushioned the stony floor around an enormous lake that gleamed the sort of sapphire blue that holiday brochures promised.

A waterfall rippled at the far side, cascading into the lake with a froth of crystal water that sparkled in the cave light.

A splash caught my eye, and I gasped as a mermaid waved

and swam over. She pulled herself out of the azure lake and I saw that she wasn't a mermaid, but rather a humanoid with pale green-blue skin that looked like it had never seen the sun and long hair that hung down her back in kelpy strands. Her face was rounded and pinkish fronds fluttered on the side of her face like bits of coral. She looked like a large axolotl with hair, and she wore a wispy dress that fell open as she moved, revealing glimpses of her rounded thighs and the side of her breasts.

"George, a pleasure as always," she said in a soft voice that rippled like the water behind her.

George bowed. "The pleasure is mine, as always." They smiled fondly at the pale woman. "I brought you an offering." They dug around in my backpack and pulled out the fish George had stored in there.

The axolotl woman smiled, showing pointed teeth as she accepted the trout and placed it on a nearby rock. "And I see you also brought a friend."

George coughed and straightened. "Dedomena, this is Elle; she's working in the Archives on a placement. Elle, this is Dedomena, guardian of our data lake."

She held out a wet hand. I shook it once before dropping it. Dedomena laughed and took a step back. This meant her webbed feet were in the water. She didn't seem to mind.

"This is incredible," I breathed, turning to take in the view again. I didn't think I'd seen anything so beautiful as this cave. "Are those diamonds?" I asked, identifying some glowing gems embedded in the rock as the light source.

Dedomena nodded. "They are. They also help keep the data pure."

I frowned in confusion and looked around. What did she mean by data?

"Do you want to see how it works?" Dedomena asked, her dark eyes gleaming.

I nodded and stepped as close as I could to the water's edge without getting my leather shoes wet.

George leaned against one of the walls and waited, a smile on their lips.

"Ask for a piece of information the company would have," Dedomena ordered, looking at me with eyes that were too large for her pointed face.

"Er…" My mind went blank. "How about personnel data? About me?" I added quickly so it didn't look like I was prying.

Dedomena laughed. "That's what everyone asks for. Alright then. Confidential personnel data it is." She walked onto the lake. I mean, she literally walked out onto the water, without sinking into it. My eyes almost came out of my head.

The diamond lights shone brighter as Dedomena turned in a slow circle, her arms held out wide and her eyes closed.

The diamonds formed beams of white light that streamed into the lake, refracting into strange angled and curved shapes that defied my knowledge of the laws of physics. But I thought I could sense some sort of order under the surface, rippling through the lights in odd fractals.

Solving that sort of equation would put me on the list for all prestigious prizes in the field of mathematics and I itched to try it, even though I knew it was beyond my abilities. This was the sort of problem people could spend lifetimes over. No one had studied magical mathematics in any detail, and this was a pinnacle of a problem.

My fingers twitched, and I longed for my notebook so I could scribble some of my thoughts down. Simple geometry was out, of course, but there must be some logic in it. My mind warred with my logical nature as my soul sang with the beauty of whatever ritual Dedomena was performing.

Now she sang, her voice as clear as the diamonds that continued to shine in the cave walls. I felt the song deep in my body.

I wanted to join her. The thought should have startled me, but it felt natural. All I had to do was step onto the lake and I could dance to her song, help her, get lost in the data.

A strong hand landed on my shoulder, preventing me from moving forwards. I looked round in frustration to see George shaking their head. Breaking eye contact with the ritual brought me back to myself and I realised my feet were wet. Entranced by Dedomena, I had stepped into the lake.

I jumped backwards, ashamed of my lapse in control and vowed to do better.

"It's alright. I'm surprised you didn't jump in. That's how we lost Simon. He's still in there somewhere. He helps with storage now."

I had no idea if they were joking.

Dedomena's song came to an end, and she pointed to a shimmering picture of me hovering above the lake. It was a whiteish blue colour, but I winced as I recognised my awful pass photo. My hand went to its copy on the badge around my neck in a reflexive gesture.

With a wave of her hand, the photograph disappeared, and my personal information shimmered there instead; date of birth, full name, address. A flick of her fingers and the name of my manager appeared, along with previous managers, length of service, performance reviews and salary.

"Satisfied?" Dedomena asked.

I nodded. It was incredible.

She waved her hand for a final time and my information wafted back into the lake. I saw the numbers and words float around for a moment before they got lost in the rippling water.

"So all the company's data is stored here?" I asked. I was aiming for intelligent interest, but my brain had cut to obvious idiotic questions.

Dedomena nodded. "Most supernatural companies have something like this. Me and my sisters are quite in demand, although some of them only have data pools." She sniffed. "This is the largest and most comprehensive data lake in Europe, and I'm putting an application together for an expansion. The company just keeps adding data, and no one listens to my requests for a clean-up. Goddess forbid a vampire ever deleted anything." She shook her head. "So expansion it is. One day I might even get the Archives logged in here."

George snorted as if that was hilarious.

"Is it only you who can access it?" I asked.

That tinkling laugh again, like a river running over pebbles. "What would be the point in that? The diamonds in the water are an interface with our intranet system for easy searching."

I peered into the pool to make out the bright jewels lining the lake under the surface. "Wow," I breathed. "And restricted data?"

"Is marked with tags, and access linked to specific nodes. I take data protection very seriously." Dedomena's open face turned sinister for a moment. Her eyes darkened to black shimmering pearls, her seaweed fronds streamed around her as if caught in a breeze, and her teeth lengthened to points. I blinked and she was back to the beautiful axolotl woman I had seen when she first emerged from the lake. "Did you want anything else?"

I looked to George, who shook their head. They held back a curtain of the trailing green plants for me, and I turned to get one last look at the amazing data lake. I'd always thought data pools and warehouses and such were just terms to describe storage, but now I'd seen this I questioned everything I'd once thought.

As we left, I looked over my shoulder to see her bending over the silver fish, blood running down her chin.

The cave felt colder than it had done and as we left, the comforting half-light of the labyrinth soothed me.

"She's something else, isn't she?" George sounded in awe, looking back through the stone archway that led to the data lake.

"What is she?"

George sighed. "A naiad or water nymph," they said with a dreamy quality to their voice before a small frown creased their forehead. "But it's rude to ask people's species."

"Sorry."

They waved away my apology. "It's alright. I suppose you need to know. They can make themselves into any form so they appear more attractive. If they really like you, they try to take you with them to their underwater homes, the water ones, anyway." Another sigh followed by a shake of the head. George's voice became sharper and less wistful. "Right, let's crack on, shall we?"

Chapter 12

Dragons are fascinating creatures that are often misunderstood. We see them from a human point of view, but they were around long before humans arrived on the scene. Some believe they are simply apex predators, but, in my experience, they are sensitive creatures who enjoy acquiring and sharing knowledge. That is one of many reasons why their primary language of Draconic is so complicated.

Aloora Dragonquest – *Talking with dragons, a comprehensive study of cases and contextualism in Draconic*

George continued on their rounds, striding through the labyrinth with no concern for moving walls or the occasional strange bumps that echoed through the halls. We checked on some of the artefacts including a book that hummed a rendition of Beethoven's fifth symphony and a tiny box that fluttered around our heads like an insect.

"Some of the artefacts stored here get fractious if we don't pay them attention. I've got a strict schedule to make sure we don't favour one over the others."

"Can they really tell if it's fair?"

George raised one thick eyebrow. I guessed that meant they could tell. "The last time we didn't visit the Grimoire of Storms for a week, the entire place got covered with fog for a month."

Next up was the restricted section.

"I like to walk at least one of the corridors each day and check nothing's escaped," George said as they held a hand up to a red crystal embedded in a shelf. I recognised the alarm light from my accident the previous day. It fluttered and turned white before flashing back to red. When they nodded, we moved forward. No alarm blared. "This part of the labyrinth holds our most precious and most dangerous items."

We both slowed as we walked this corridor. Maybe it was my imagination, but a thick layer of ominousness spread over this section. Something about the arrangement of a shelf looked familiar. I paused to study it. "This was where I was yesterday."

George nodded. "You shouldn't have been able to get this far. Thank the labyrinth that the pressure alarms still worked." They pointed to the floor.

I bent to study the smooth tiles. They all looked the same to me.

"Some of these stones have pressure sensors under them. It's rudimentary, but it works for anyone who can break through the wards. The alarm attracts…other protections we have and of course myself and Ahmed."

"So, if we stood on it now?"

"I've disabled the alarm."

"With the crystal?" I asked to show I'd paid attention.

That observation earned me a nod of approval. "There is a route through, of course, but it's easier to just turn the alarm off while we're on our rounds because I can never remember the exact order you need to step in and the sequence is affected by moon phases and the Aztec calendar and whatever else Ahmed could think of."

I nodded.

George turned serious. Shadows stretched across their face as they looked down at me. "There's serious stuff here, Elle. Do not try to wander around here by yourself. Some of these items are cursed, some are just ruddy dangerous. Look." They pointed to a copper-coloured sword that glinted wickedly under the lights. "This is Dyrnwyn." As their hand got close to the blade, a ripple of flame licked over the sword, as if tasting the air. "It burns with supernatural fire. If a worthy person wields it, the fire helps them with their cause, but if it doesn't judge them as worthy, the flames consume them."

"How does a sword decide what's worthy?"

George shrugged. "No idea." They moved their hand away. The sword dulled back to a coppery red. "I wouldn't want to risk being judged by an inanimate object. And over there is a sheaf of Cupid's arrows."

I walked over to examine the arrows.

George's hand gripped my wrist. "Do not touch them. I do not want you to become obsessed with me."

I looked over my shoulder at George. They were serious.

"You touch one of the heads and you fall in love with the next person you see. There's no known cure."

"Why are they here?"

George lifted a shoulder. "Not for us to ask questions like that. We just store them. The legal department and Ahmed work out the contracts. Sometimes we get the risk assessors involved, but I've never known us to refuse to take an item. Well, maybe if there was a risk of one of the old gods coming down here."

I backed away from the arrows. "OK, don't touch anything in the restricted section. Got it."

"Good." George nodded, then ran a hand over their face. "I don't mean to be stern, but don't come in here on your own. Ahmed's reset all the protections, but just, stay away from this section unless you're with one of us. It's really important, Elle. I know you graduates are all keen to impress, but trust me, don't try to get in here on your own."

"I won't." I didn't want to accidentally fall in love with anyone or get cursed. It already felt like my life was hard enough trying to juggle my career, pay off my overdraft and manage whatever neurosis I had, so I didn't need seven years bad luck on top of that. Or worse. I wrapped my arms around myself.

Glancing around, I saw another sword. This one was more

worn than Dyrnwen, with a duller blade and the remains of gold flecks around its pommel.

"Shouldn't we keep the swords together?" My logical brain craved order.

George followed my gaze and shook his head. "Some of the artefacts don't play well together. I started out storing by type of object, but once you've been in the middle of two enchanted weapons fighting it out, you learn to keep them apart before you get your head chopped off. Excalibur doesn't like anything else outshining it, so it stays here next to the jewels."

"That's Excalibur." My eyes became round. The real sword of King Arthur lay in front of me. I could reach out and touch it. I hadn't spent a lot of time reading myths and legends as a child, but one of my foster families had a daughter who loved anything Arthurian, and some of it had stuck with me through the trips to Glastonbury and the bedtime stories about knights and damsels in distress.

She would love to see this. A soft pang of longing shot through my heart. It was a shame the family had moved abroad for the dad's work. I liked them more than most of my foster families and they were good people, didn't treat me like a second-class child and they never talked down to me. They were academics who supported my maths studies, even allowing me to sign up for my double maths GCSEs early. I sighed. Would my life have been different if they hadn't moved? Could I have stayed with them and had a more settled childhood?

My hand strayed to my Lilo and Stitch watch as I ran through what ifs…what if the family who'd gifted me the watch as an early seventh birthday present hadn't had that car accident and had adopted me? What if I had been a better daughter to the subsequent foster families so they wanted to keep me? What if I'd worked harder and gotten a hundred percent in my Year 9 maths quiz?

Sums. Sums would help. A compulsion seized me. I had to tap out the answer to seven times seven. But George was watching me. I knew from experience that ignoring the compulsion would make it stronger, and soon I'd have to tap out seven cubed to soothe my stupid brain. I tapped my index finger against the nearest shelf, moving my body to block George's view of my crazy as I did forty-nine taps as fast as possible. Once I'd finished, I let out a sigh of relief.

"You good?" asked George with a look of concern on their cow-like face.

I nodded, pushing all thoughts of family down. I had to focus on my work, not moon after a family I couldn't have.

"OK, so today, we're going to check on our newest acquisition."

"The Crown of Winter?" I asked.

George nodded and took out a notebook; hot pink leather covering with fluffy feathers along the edges, lined paper inside filled with scribbled writing. Looks like I wasn't the only one who liked a unique notebook. They read out a number and we crept along the corridor in silence, checking boxes until we came to the familiar wooden one that housed the Crown of Winter.

George made a note and touched the box with the end of their biro before sprinkling some powder over it. The powder looked suspiciously like gold glitter. "Magic detection dust," they said, narrowing their eyes at the box. "No one's touched this since it came in and the protections the emperor put there are still in place." With a nod we moved on.

"Now it's time to feed the dragon."

I stopped dead in my tracks. My heart skipped a beat. "Dragon?" Was that a joke?

George had carried on and turned a corner, leaving me alone in the labyrinth. I ran forwards to catch up and skidded to a halt, slamming into George's back where they'd stopped.

In front of a dragon.

I blinked, clearing my eyes, willing them to make sense of what they saw. Because somehow, among the narrow corridors of the labyrinth was a large red dragon. Its scales gleamed under the soft light, giving its coat a burnished jewelled finish that reminded me of faded rubies.

It shifted its huge feet, and I noticed the heap of boxes it sat on.

"Morning, Xam," George said. "I've brought you some breakfast."

The dragon watched us with enormous eyes the colour of quicksilver. George heaved their rucksack off their back and pulled out an enormous hunk of meat, which they threw in front of the dragon.

The creature ignored the offering and tilted its head to one side, studying me.

George looked over their shoulder. "This is Elle; she's working with us. She is not to be harmed."

Welcome, Elle. I am Xamianthazyrsbc. You may call me Xam.

The voice sounded in my head without going through my ears. I gaped. "It spoke."

Of course. And I am a she, not an it.

"Sorry, sorry. I've never spoken to a dragon before."

The dragon made a coughing sound that might have been a laugh.

"How are you down here?"

I choose to stay here. It is a sacred duty to protect such knowledge. The dragon moved again, and a few books slid slowly down the pile it sat on.

"Anything to report?" George asked, their notebook out.

The dragon shook its head.

"Do you need anything?"

A copy of Homer's Margites.

"You know we don't have that here."

A dragon can dream. Then, no, nothing. Be off with you.

We backed away.

I waited until I thought we were out of earshot before I asked, "How is a dragon down here?"

George looked up from their notebook, and squinted at me as if they had just remembered I was here. "Xam turned up one day not too long ago, just after the first dragons came back into the world – did you see the mess they made of Cardiff?" I nodded. It had been all over the news when they'd nested in the Millenium Stadium. George shook their head. "Anyway, she offered to help us guard what we have here in exchange for access to any books. We were reticent at first, but Ahmed came to an agreement with her – watch out making bargains with him, he's as tricky as a fae – so here she is; a valuable addition to our security."

"She was sitting on books."

"Dragons like hoarding things. At least, she does. And she takes care of them. If you can't find a rare book that should be in the Archives, check with Xam."

Something else bothered me. "That food you gave her…" George waited politely as I found the question I wanted to ask. "It doesn't look like enough for her size…"

They took pity on me. "I don't understand it fully, but she gets most of her nutrition from the magic and knowledge down here. We feed her at least once a day though and, if anyone does manage to break into the Archives, she gets a bit more fresh meat in her diet."

Another joke? George didn't laugh. I thought back to the flicker of flames when I had wandered into the restricted section and shrank back as if I could feel the heat on my skin now. Xam could have eaten me.

"Right, let's carry on then." George led the way to the next stop on the tour.

~

It had been a long morning that had turned into early afternoon before George declared their rounds finished for the day. They showed me three pages of crossed off items in their pink notebook to confirm we were done and sent me off for a late lunch.

I checked my emails, confirming that I'd missed the other graduates who had taken lunch together, and set off to eat my sandwiches alone. I had suggested I could eat at my desk and keep working but George had given me a look of horror at the thought of getting crumbs anywhere near the Archives, so I'd retreated upstairs.

On my way back down, I heard voices as soon as I left the lift.

"Walked right through the ward." That was George's voice. I frowned. Had there been a break in? The labyrinth was meant to be impenetrable.

George and Ahmed were speaking to a third figure who had their back to me. There was something familiar about the set of their shoulders and aura of general power and control. As I approached, I heard more snatches of their conversation.

"…totally null. Have you heard of anything like it?" Ahmed asked.

"I did wonder." The figure cut off whatever he was about to say next and turned his gaze on me. "Ah, here she is." It was my mentor, Newton.

I smiled nervously, unsure what to do. It was clear they were in the middle of a private conversation, one they didn't want me to overhear. Oh no, was I the null?

I might not be a stellar performer in the Archives, but I didn't think I was that bad. And I'd only been here for a couple of days so I hadn't had time to mess anything up. My stomach twisted as I thought of my performance review. It was a feature of the graduate scheme that there weren't enough jobs at the end for all of us who started. A negative placement review could scupper any chance I had at getting a permanent role and becoming the director of my own department before I was thirty. The smile on my face became brittle.

I had to keep my composure. Letting any emotions show would only worsen my case. Straightening my spine, I walked past them to my station in the Archives, unlocked my laptop and stared at the screen, not seeing the new emails or the lines of the database proposal I was working on.

Two sets of eyes bored into me as I pretended to work. They were definitely talking about me. Schiztz. And now things were so bad, I was using Dwarfish curse words in my head.

Newton gave a polite cough. "And how is your second

placement coming along?

"Good, I think," I replied, shooting a look at Ahmed for confirmation.

The djinni gave nothing away as he regarded me, arms folded over a new waistcoat. This one had a pattern of books edged with copper thread. "It has been two days."

"Time flies when you are enjoying yourself, or so Einstein said. I do wish I had been the one to so elegantly document the theory of relativity, but my focus at the time was in other areas."

I blinked at Newton's words. I shouldn't be surprised. My mentor was a genius, that's right, he was that Isaac Newton, the one with the laws of motion and gravitation, although I hadn't worked up the courage to ask if the story about the apple was true.

"And speaking of focus in other areas, do you have that Greek treaty on mighty Helios?"

"The sun?" I asked.

"Indeed. It is an ongoing line of inquiry that I continue to explore." His gaze turned wistful. "Ever since becoming…afflicted…by vampirism, I have yearned for the warmth of sweet sunlight upon my face. But alas, as rosy-fingered dawn enters the world, so I must retreat inside. And yet," his red eyes lit with excitement, "what is the moon but a reflection of sunlight on a lump of rock far from us? So, perhaps it is not impossible to go out in the light of day without such protection as I must wear currently. That is my current focus."

"You want vampires to be daywalkers?" I asked.

"Exactly so. And thus avoid the horrors of having to carry a parasol or an oversized hat." Newton nodded. "And as I have always found I have made my discoveries by standing on the shoulders of giants who have gone before me, I have decided to look far back into our histories to see what the learned Greeks had to say for themselves."

"Here." Ahmed handed over a small volume with a sniff. "But why you think Aristarchus of Samos can help, I do not know. I knew Samos back then, and it spat out crazy philosophers like flies. Pythagoras forbade people from eating the beans, for goodness' sake."

"Ah, well, it helps to study diverse writings, and I do not believe Aristarchus had the same problem with legumes." Newton took the book and gave a tiny bow. "Good day to you, Mr Ahmed, Miss Bruma and Mx George."

Chapter 13

Supernaturals ain't natural

Anti-Magic League Slogan

The rest of my first fortnight at the Archives passed quickly as I researched databases and categorisation systems with RFID tags and barcodes in between helping George with their rounds. Everything other than a manual cataloguing was expensive, assuming you didn't count my labour as a cost, which I didn't. I was here to work, and I'd do that, regardless. I needed to make my mark on this department so nobody thought of me as 'null' and after a couple of weeks of extensive research, I was ready.

I pulled together my findings into a presentation and prepared to present to Ahmed and George. They sat on a couple of comfy leather armchairs that Ahmed had conjured and waited. George leaned forward and smiled, encouraging me, while Ahmed had a look of bored amusement on his face as he twiddled with one drooping moustache.

I coughed, both chills and hot prickles running over my body at the attention. Even though it was just the two of them, the familiar sickness swelled in my stomach at the thought of giving a formal presentation.

I went through my preparation steps; deep breathing, think of it like a normal conversation. The slides I had created were simply to illustrate my points, not an indicator of a formal presentation. The roiling sensation in my stomach calmed a little, but my hands still shook as I enlarged the slides so they covered the full screen and started my presentation; *Bringing the Archives into the new millennium.*

I liked the title, but Ahmed shifted in his seat. "Remind me which millennium we're in now?"

"The third, in the common era, if you use mundane human historical dating," George answered with a smile at me and a gesture to carry on.

I inhaled a deep breath and started, "While numbering systems may have been sufficient in the past, nowadays there are more options for tracking collections, so, rather than relying on the brain power of the cataloguer or faded ink in a record book, we can reduce key man – I mean, key djinni and minotaur – dependency by digitising the system."

I brought up the example I'd created. "This is a simple example, to get the idea. It's not fully developed, and–" I cut myself off and clenched my hands into balls. I was not apologising. This was a prototype. "So, if say, someone needed to find the Crown of Winter or item seven hundred thousand, four hundred and sixty-two, then I could type it in here in the search function on either name, or number or, when developed, keywords, and it would bring up the reference number for the location in the Archives, saving time."

George clapped with more enthusiasm than the idea merited.

Ahmed paused in twirling his moustache. "But why do we need this, when we have everything in a catalogue?" The humongous book appeared in his lap, and he patted it.

I coughed. "When I examined the earliest entries, I found the ink had faded and it was unclear what had been retrieved and what still remained in the Archives."

"That's only a problem for mortals without a keen memory." He looked around. "Now, where did I put my tea?"

George passed him the cup and shot me a wink. "It's a shame we didn't have something like this in place before the last sighting of Halley's Comet. You could have tracked its progress, like you wanted, instead of being stuck here…the only one who knows where everything is."

Ahmed sipped his tea and sighed. "It would be nice to leave the Archives sometimes, I suppose. I do yearn for the feel of desert winds against my skin, and you cannot beat the thrill of dune racing."

"If you had the catalogue digitised, then you could leave someone else here while you took a holiday." I pressed on.

"I'm happy to do it. The most basic barcode system would cost approximately twenty-five pence per label plus the software and reader costs or, I could build a database with Dedomena's support." The reference number of the latest entry into the Archives weighed on my mind. "I could start it, anyway. It would be my way of trying to improve things while I'm here."

"I suppose it would keep you occupied. There is not much else you can do here. And, if we do not get on with it, we can always shut it down."

"That's the spirit," said George, beaming.

"A trial, then." Ahmed raised his teacup to me in a toast.

I smiled, hoping my face didn't give away my disappointment. I could spend months on this, and they would just delete it if they didn't like it. But, I squared my shoulders, at least Ahmed had agreed to try it. Now I would just have to prove it was a good investment.

Buoyed by my success, I was looking forward to a night out with the other graduates. In the safety of the ladies' bathroom in the basement, I took a crumpled dress out of my bag and scowled at it.

Why had I trusted my flatmate's breezy comment that it would be fine and not put it in a suit protector? Yes, they were bulkier, but at least my dress wouldn't look as wrinkly as an elephant's scrotum. That was what I got for trying to 'chill out'. My heart rate spiked. I pressed my back against the cool bathroom tiles and slowed my breathing. It wasn't too late to back out. I could spend the night at our flat, maybe order some Thai food, and our oven probably needed a good clean. Now I just had to think of a good excuse…I could say my hamster was ill, or I was ill, or–

"Wotcher, Elle." Precious' voice interrupted my excuses.

"What are you doing here?"

"Getting ready. Same as you. No one uses these loos, they're too out of the way. Nice dress. That fabric doesn't show the creases."

"Actually, I'm not feeling great."

Precious looked me up and down. "You don't want to come."

She'd seen through me in the space of one blink of her large eyes. "We-ell…"

"I get it. A lot of our co-workers are dicks. But we can ditch them after a couple of drinks."

That didn't sound too bad, and I could go home when Precious left; she'd give me the perfect excuse. I picked up my rumpled dress. She was right; the fabric didn't show the creases too much. "OK."

Precious gave me a broad grin and shimmied out of her suit before reaching into an oversized handbag and pulling out a scrap of fabric. Embarrassed by her body confidence, I retreated to a cubicle to get changed and only banged my elbow against the walls twice.

When I left the toilet, Precious had transformed into an orc ready to party. The swatch of purple fabric turned out to be a bodycon dress that came to her thighs, and she'd changed out of her work heels and into over the knee leather boots.

"They've got room for my dirk," she said, pulling out her dagger to show me. She twirled it in her palm before re-holstering it somewhere in the depth of her boot.

"You'll have to teach me how to do that," I said with admiration as I leaned forward to apply some lipstick to my pale face.

"It's easy." The knife appeared back in her hand. "The key is confidence and practice." She offered me the blade.

"Isn't that a family heirloom?"

She shrugged. "It's not like you're going to steal it." Precious let out a snort of laughter and my pride twinged. Of course I would never dream of stealing from anyone, let alone my best work friend, but she'd insinuated I didn't have a chance of beating her in a fight. I didn't, but my pride was still hurt.

I took the dagger and tried a twirl. It slipped from my grasp and fell to the floor with a clang followed by a loud crack.

I stared with mounting horror at the broken tile.

Precious bent and scooped up her knife.

"What have I done? Should I tell someone? I should tell someone."

"Elle." Precious gave me a look. "I'm not going to tell anyone, and neither should you."

"But–"

"But nothing. It was an accident. No one will know it was you. You worry too much. Besides, I don't want to give them any chance to confiscate my clan dirk." Her eyes were wide with pleading.

It was her vulnerability that made my mind up. "Alright."

"You're a sport." She punched me on the arm, and I rubbed the spot, sure it was going to bruise. "Now, let's go before someone comes in." My eyes widened, and she snorted. "Kidding."

I finished getting ready at double speed and soon we were up in the atrium, ready to leave the building and head to the pub nearby for drinks.

Precious rolled her shoulders. "I cannot wait to get away from some of the pretentious gits I work with."

"Hello ladies." With unerring timing, Tristan appeared behind us and slung his arms around our shoulders.

Precious caught my eye and we burst out into giggles.

"Let me in on the joke," Tristan said, eyeing Precious' mouth.

I shook my head, gasping for breath.

"Talking about you, not to you," Precious taunted.

A senior vampire narrowed his eyes at us as he entered the building for the night shift. The Bathory Corporation was a twenty-four-hour operation.

I bit my lip to stop the laughter, and we hurried out of the front doors before the vampire decided they needed a snack. A gaggle of protestors sat on the pavement outside the head office. When they saw Precious' green skin, they did a double take and stood, clutching homemade signs that said things like 'Go Home' and 'We don't need no supernaturals'.

Precious' jaw twitched and she stiffened her spine. I linked my arm through hers and held my head high.

"Stop taking our jobs!" screamed one man, coming close to our group.

Precious growled and he took a step back.

"Did you see that? She threatened me!"

Cries of support rang through the small group of protesters, and someone got out a mobile phone and started filming. Tristan got his own smartphone out and filmed them back.

They didn't like that.

"What are you, some sort of troll-lover?"

"Jealous?" asked Tristan, winding his arm around Precious' waist.

She pulled away. "I'm an orc, you imbecile," Precious said with a low undercurrent of menace.

We passed through to more shaking of signs and general jeering. I kept my gaze straight ahead, avoiding eye contact.

"Is it just me, or are there more of them lately?" I asked once we were far enough away that I felt safe.

Precious slumped down onto a bench, pulling me down with her as my arm was still linked through hers. She held her head in her hands for a moment before rubbing her face and sucking in a deep breath. "I don't know if there are more of them or if they've just got louder. There's always idiots who hate people like me just for existing."

I shuffled my feet. I had no idea what it felt like to be an orc. Or any supernatural. I was a regular, no power human.

Precious shook her head and got to her feet with purpose. "Right, I need a drink. First round's on Tristan."

She stomped off and we raced to keep up as she made her way to the Bathory Corporation's unofficial drinking hole and closest pub; the Pickled Winkle.

Chapter 14

Relaxation is important. When you've lived through a few centuries, you realise how easy it is to burn out trying to experience and achieve everything at once. One of the benefits of longevity is that it gives you perspective.

Elizabeth Bathory – *The First Disrupter*

The Pickled Winkle was a traditional pub with dark beams, a muddy paint job on the wall behind framed vintage beermats, and lots of shady booths that people could hide in. It wasn't welcoming, but it had old school pricing and didn't ask questions or turn away supernaturals, and it was close to the office, so we'd adopted it as our local.

In the pub, Tristan got the first round while Precious and I found a table in the corner. The pub was almost full, as most pubs are in London on a Friday night, and a low hum of conversation greeted us. A few people looked up when we went in and I stepped closer to Precious to show my support. Not that she needed it. She strode through the bar to an empty table as if she owned the place. I could almost believe she was fine after the earlier encounter.

Except that, when Tristan joined us with the drinks, Precious downed half of her glass of wine in one go.

"Woah there, slow down," said Tristan. "Someone might take advantage of you if you get bladdered."

Precious curled her lip and drank the rest of her wine without taking her eyes off him. A drip escaped her lips and trickled down her chin. She wiped it away with her thumb then sucked it clean. Tristan's gaze stayed on her sucking her thumb and his mouth fell open until he looked like one of the plastic fish hung on the wall.

"No one takes advantage of me," Precious said.

I snorted into my glass of rum and coke at her put down. Tristan needed his confidence taking down a peg or two and I loved seeing Precious do it.

A few other graduates I recognised from the scheme joined us, crowding round the table.

"You've fallen behind." Precious headed to the bar and ordered another round, plonking the glasses on the table when she returned.

She downed her second glass and eyed us like she expected us to keep up.

Tristan caught my eye before shrugging his shoulders. "Bottom's up." He took a long swig of his pint. "Did you hear about Lucy?"

I shook my head. Precious stared at a trout on the wall.

"She got fired for damaging team morale with a sticker chart. I heard she got fifteen complaints about her and it was so bad it was going to impact the employee survey results, so they let her go."

"I thought she was running one of the nightclubs?" I asked.

Precious stood up, causing my drink to slosh over the side of the glass. I mopped at the spill with a beermat. "Good idea. We should go to a nightclub."

"We just got here," Tristan protested.

"I don't know…" I didn't want a big night out. I'd planned to have a couple of drinks, make my excuses and head home. I had a mountain of studying to do this weekend as well as my usual cleaning routine in our flat and I didn't want to tackle either with a hangover. But then I saw the look in Precious' dark eyes; haunted and in need of escape. It was an expression I knew well; I'd seen it often enough in the mirror.

"How about Blud?" I suggested. It was the only supernatural bar I knew, and I didn't want Precious to have to deal with any stupid humans tonight.

"You want us to go to a bar owned by our employer?" Tristan shook his head at me like I was stupid.

No. I did not want to go there. Last time I'd been in a club, a vampire had tried to feel me up, but for Precious, I'd pull up my big girl pants and do it. "Ye-es," I stammered.

"Let's go." And Precious was already out the door.

And like that, we were on the tube to the fashionable part of London where the flagship Blud nightclub sat bathed in red light from its neon blood drop sign. They eyed the work badge I'd hung back around my neck and waved us in. No queuing for Bathory Corporation employees.

Inside, and I knew this was a bad idea. Blud was only half full – it was still early by nocturnal supernatural standards – but the music was loud, and the lights were low. A trio of attractive vampire bartenders mixed cocktails behind the copper bar while a mixture of supernaturals and humans who liked the vampire mystique gyrated on the dance floor and others sat on tall stools next to narrow copper tables.

A blonde hung over the bar trying to catch the eye of one of the bartenders with her cleavage as she stroked her neck, drawing attention to her jugular. My entire body tensed as I relived the last time I was here. Was the vampire who'd pressed me up against the wall in a case of mistaken identity here tonight?

I shuddered. Some people might get off on being a juice box but, for me, it was one of the worst parts of working at the Bathory Corporation, knowing you could be called on to donate blood to a hungry vampire. I was lucky that they didn't pick on me too much, favouring meals that didn't require a trip down to the Archives. Besides, every vampire that had snacked on me said I tasted awful.

Precious and Tristan disappeared off to get drinks while I

nabbed one of the tall tables. It came up to my chest so I couldn't even lean on the darned thing, but it was the only free table in the place. I managed to grab some chairs with spindly metal legs and fiddled with arranging them as I attempted to relax.

Of course, that made me even clumsier and I managed to knock into the next table, sending a pint of beer flying.

"I'm so sorry," I said, reaching out to mop up the spillage with the tiny napkin left on my table. The music pulsed around us, just too loud to let people talk at a normal volume but too soft to hear the words to the song clearly.

A bloke with beer breath and tight jeans – now soaked in booze – stood and stared me down. "These were new jeans," he shouted over the music.

"S-sorry," I repeated.

"And that was a full pint."

"Yep, sorry about that. I'll get you a new one."

"And what about my jeans? I can't take them off here."

"Not if you don't want to get arrested." I attempted to joke. It landed flat as a 2D shape.

"Is there a problem here?" a familiar voice said.

I looked up to see Liam standing in the club, a vision in a dark shirt with fitted black jeans.

The man with wet jeans grabbed my wrist tight. He was so close, I could smell his bad beer breath as he spoke. "No problem. She was just about to buy me a new pint."

"Yes, sure. Absolutely. What are you having?" I tried to get out of his grip, but he held tight.

"Let her go." Liam frowned and stepped forward.

Before he could do anything, Precious appeared like a warrior queen. She moved in close, stepping between Liam and Bad Breath. The orc slammed her fist down on Bad Breath's wrist, jarring him enough to release me. I stepped back, clutching my arm, still red from his sticky fingers, and watched as she brought his arm behind his back in a tight hold.

"Everything alright here," Precious said. It wasn't a question.

Liam slapped down a couple of twenties on the table, right in the middle of the puddle of beer that I hadn't been able to mop up. "This should cover the drink and cleaning for your jeans."

The man screwed up his face, unsure whether to take the cash or continue making an issue of me spilling his pint. Precious tightened her hold, and he nodded.

Liam leaned forward and lowered his voice. "You might want to get those jeans off quick. I heard that a guy sat in wet jeans all day and ended up getting his balls stuck. He had to go to A&E to get the trousers cut off."

The man winced, whether from the thought of getting stuck in his jeans or Precious' grip, I didn't know, but as soon as Precious released him, he swiped the cash and left the bar.

"I wish I could do that," I said staring after the man.

"I can teach you. Monday. Now let's dance." Precious

moved her hips in time with the music, the groaning man forgotten. She grabbed me so I moved with her, Liam swaying in time behind me. I didn't even think to ask why he was in the vampire bar, it felt natural that he joined us.

Precious didn't even bat an eyelid when Tristan joined us, almost, but not quite grinding against her hip.

I left them to it and headed for a table while Liam made it to the bar. He plonked a bottle of lager in front of me and chinked it with his own.

"Cheers," he said.

"Thanks for…you know."

He brushed off my thanks and studied me with those warm eyes. "Are you OK?"

"Sure." But I would book in a counselling session tomorrow. I tapped the beer bottle against the glass tabletop seven times as if that could make up for years of therapy and solve all my problems. It didn't, but it gave my brain some relief from the compulsion.

Liam frowned at his bottle.

"Something on your mind?" I asked. It was easier to focus on him than on me.

"What do you think of this?" He pulled out his phone and showed me a picture of a puzzle box. Our fingers brushed, sending a jolt of heat through me as I held the phone steady so I could get a closer look.

"Looks interesting," I managed to breathe out.

"Right? And this?" He swiped to another picture of a lego set of a bunch of flowers. "What would you think if someone got you these as a Christmas present?"

"A bunch of flowers and all the fun of building them? Yes, please." I kept the tone light, trying to avoid thinking about how close we were, how attractive he looked when he played with his glasses and how his fingers still touched mine as we stared at his phone. Where was this going?

"I know, right?" He sighed and took a swig of his beer.

"Did someone get you those for Christmas?"

Liam laughed. "No, that's what I got Rani. But she went spare, said I didn't understand her and she'd hinted at a charm bracelet. She didn't even try to open the box."

I winced. "You hid the bracelet in there?"

"Got it in one." He raised his bottle to me. "You get it."

"What happened?" I had to know.

"We argued–"

"Hey, what was your degree in?" Tristan barged his way into the conversation.

"Er, maths." What did that had to do with anything?

Precious laughed. "Told you."

"What?" I asked.

"Tristan's upset because he's got a useless degree."

"Art history is not useless."

"Sure," replied Precious, dragging out the word.

"Alright. If your degree is so good, tell me a maths fact."

Why was he picking on me? Precious was the one who said he had a rubbish degree. But I did know a lot of maths facts and maybe I could win back Liam's money after he bailed me out with the troll-breath tight-jeans guy. "OK, I bet you fifty quid that the circumference of that pint glass is longer than the height."

Tristan squinted at the glass. "No way. It's taller than it is across."

"Across is the diameter," I explained. "Circumference is all the way around the edge."

"It's still taller."

I grinned. "Nope. Circumference is πD. D is diameter," I spelled it out for him. His eyebrows drew together in confusion. "So if we take π as three point one four or three if that's easier then you can see that three times the diameter is taller than the height." I used my thumb and forefinger to measure the diameter and then held it next to the pint glass by the base and twisted my hand twice to show him.

"Blow me," he said, amazed.

"You wish," Precious shot back.

Tristan got out his phone to check my maths, repeated my thumb and forefinger measuring before handing me over a fifty-pound note.

I stared at it. I'd never seen one in person before. I ran my fingers over the note, reminding myself that I wasn't a poor student anymore before handing it to Liam. "To cover that guy's cleaning bill."

Liam clinked his beer bottle against mine and grinned. "To maths."

That was a toast I could get on board with. I drank, blaming the warm tingly feeling in my stomach on the alcohol and definitely not on the way Liam looked at me or how he leaned in when he talked, as if he wanted to get closer to me. I wanted to ask him more about the argument.

"Let's get out of here." Tristan appeared between us, snagged my bottle and downed it, cutting off any chance of a conversation with Liam.

Precious tugged me upright and we left without a plan about where to go next. On the way to wherever we were heading, Tristan explained what had happened with Lucy in more detail. Apparently, she'd tried to change some of the feeding rules for the vampire staff and introduced a sticker chart. Needless to say, that hadn't gone down well. After a lot of complaints from the bar staff, they decided to ignore the yellow badge rule and had fed on her until she was too weak to go into work. The vampires were given a slap on the wrist, but Lucy had missed too much work and was asked to leave.

"That's so unfair," I said, pulling my jacket close against the night air.

"That's the Bathory Corporation," Liam replied with a bitter edge to his baritone voice.

"I don't want to talk about work." Precious ended that conversation before I could ask Liam what he meant.

There must be some universal law that when drunk and, on a night out in London, a karaoke bar that you never knew was there during the daytime suddenly sprang to life, calling all inebriated people with the siren song of pop music, neon lighting and bad singing. Caught in its lure, we wandered inside, and Precious strode over to the stage to add her name to the list for the night.

I sat at a dark table and watched as Precious sang while I nursed my drink – some pink concoction that Tristan had bought a jug of because it was on offer. She had a great voice – good enough to be a popstar to my drunken ears – and I wondered if she was part siren, the way the punters stopped talking and watched her.

I couldn't face getting up on stage, let alone singing in front of all those people, even if the crowd was all in various stages of drunkenness. Instead, Liam and I made easy small talk while Tristan gazed up at the stage like Precious was a goddess, before joining her for a duet.

When I called it a night, Precious was on stage belting out a ballad with Tristan.

Liam insisted on seeing me to an Uber before I left, and I was so drunk I leaned in and planted a kiss on his lips before I got in.

"Sorry," I mumbled, heat blooming on my cheeks. He had a girlfriend.

"No need to apologise," he said, holding the door open for me.

"I don't…I'm not…I wouldn't…you have a girlfriend."

Liam closed the door. I wound down the window to apologise again.

"I don't have a girlfriend. I broke it off with her."

I wanted to ask more, but the driver chose that moment to speed off, leaving me with more questions than my addled brain could cope with.

Chapter 15

A free counselling service is available to all employees.

Bathory Corporation Employee Handbook

I dialled the number of the Bathory Corporation's counselling service and listened to it ring. Maybe I shouldn't call.

Nibbles, my massive hamster, gave me a reproachful look from his cage as he munched on a carrot. He was right. I should do this.

"Good morning, this is the Bathory Corporation counselling service. May I have your employee ID number?"

I reeled off the number I'd memorised. This was a confidential service, but they needed to confirm it was a genuine employee calling. "Can I speak to Jesse, please?"

The voice went silent for a moment. "We do not usually assign named counsellors."

"Please? They really helped me last time."

"I'll see what I can do." The voice was replaced by a tinny version of some classical music as they put me on hold. After a little while, a neutral voice I recognised as Jesse's spoke, "Hello?"

"Hi Jesse, it's me, Elle, I mean Abby." I remembered too late that I'd used a fake name last time I'd called up.

"I see. And how can I help you today?"

They didn't remember me. "I was the one who got attacked by a squid monster in the fae realm while on an audit."

I heard them blow out a breath. "Right. Gosh. Yeah, that was…unusual," they recovered their composure, "so have you been attacked by any more monsters at work?"

"No." No one apart from the vampires and I'd signed the employment contract that allowed them to drink my blood.

"Then how can I help you today?"

"I…" The drunken kiss with Liam loomed in my mind. It had been nothing, a mere brush of lips, but did it mean something? I had to build up to that. "I was at a club last night and a man grabbed my wrist."

"I see. How did that make you feel?" Typical therapist-style response.

"Weak, powerless. My friend had to step in to save me."

"And you resent them?"

"Precious? No! She's amazing. I wish I could be more like her."

"And how do you see her?"

"Powerful, strong." Able to stand up for herself. If I had half her confidence, I could run the Archives department.

"And what could you do to feel more like that?"

"I…don't know." I'd have to give that some thought. I scribbled it down in my new counselling notebook; Be more like Precious. It looked so easy printed on the blank page like that.

"You have the power to change," said Jesse.

"Maybe…" I'd had a lifetime of being me. The thought of changing into someone else was unsettling.

"And remember, whatever you do, you're still you. You control your actions and your mind."

I almost laughed. If I could control my mind, I could get rid of the obsessive thoughts that bubbled up and the inevitable compulsions that followed.

"I can email you some websites about empowerment if you give me your email."

It couldn't hurt. I handed over my personal email address. I'd already blown my fake name cover, I didn't want anyone at work knowing about these counselling sessions. Could Dedomena, the data nymph read my emails? What about Liam? He worked in IT after all…and that brought us back to Liam…

"Was there anything else you wanted to talk about today?"

"I might have done something stupid."

"Care to elaborate?"

"No."

"Then there's not much I can do to help except to remind you that things often seem worse than they are."

"I kissed a coworker," I blurted out.

"Wow. That was not what I was expecting. Your corporate life is a real roller coaster."

"Are you meant to say things like that?"

"Sorry," said Jesse. "It's just I've never had a client like you." They coughed. "Right. Well, there are guidelines about employee relationships. Was it a consensual kiss?"

I grimaced. I'd launched myself at him while getting into a car. That was hardly consensual. "I was sort of drunk…"

"Ah."

"The thing is, I like him. But I've really messed things up." What if he reported me to HR? That could mess up my career before it began. I skirted away from any feelings I might have for him, it was easier to focus on my career.

"Have you tried talking to him?"

"Are you mad? What if he hates me?"

"What if he likes you?" countered Jesse.

"You sound like my flatmate," I groaned.

"They sound like a very wise person."

"They are." Being an online agony aunt, Abby had a lot of insights into people problems. She was the one who prompted me to call the counselling service. "So you think I should talk to him?"

"Yes. And read the employee handbook if you start dating more seriously. And make sure any future kisses are consensual."

Good advice. I wrote that down in my notebook, too.

"Is there anything else you'd like to cover today?" Jesse asked.

"I think that's enough." I hung up, shut the notebook and stared at the motto on the front for a moment; *Your crazy is good crazy*. That had been why I'd chosen this notebook for my counselling sessions, but now I just felt loopy.

Cleaning. Cleaning would help. How could anything be wrong if everything was in the right place and sparkling clean? Where was that furniture polish?

Chapter 16

I don't deal with relationships. They are a distraction.

Elizabeth Bathory – *The First Disruptor*

"**Y**ou need to lighten up." A vampire I recognised from my stint in Foreign Audits, shoved his hands in his trouser pockets and huffed his way across the atrium towards me.

It wasn't my fault I was lost in thought. That drunken kiss with Liam had played on my mind all weekend and led to so much stress cleaning that my flatmate, Abby, had told me that if I didn't stop, she'd break the ancient vacuum cleaner that had come with the flat.

Romance wasn't in my ten-year plan, and neither were mistakes. My head told me that the kiss was a byproduct of too much alcohol and a thank you for helping rescue me from the lout at Blud. But my heart had fluttered like it had meant something and now I had to avoid the IT department because

I was too embarrassed. It was unprofessional. Liam was a colleague. Nothing more. I couldn't let anything distract me from my career right now, but my traitorous heart told me that this was one distraction it might want.

I kept my gaze on the floor, not wanting to attract the vampire's attention as I made my way to the canteen for lunch. It didn't work.

"Elle, isn't it?" he said with forced jollity. "Played with any more printers?"

Would that mishap follow me around for the rest of my career? It wasn't my fault that my supervisor had tricked me into annoying the possessed printed which had responded by dousing me with toner.

"Elle!" Liam's voice rang across the atrium. Dzrak. I'd had some half hope that he'd been so drunk he'd forgotten the kiss had even happened. From the smile he shot me, I had no such luck.

"Fred," I said, remembering the vampire's name. "How's it going with the audits?" I picked the lesser of two evils, hoping that if Liam saw me in conversation with someone else, he'd leave me alone so I didn't have to confront the fact that I'd kissed him.

"Good, good. We had to redo that asset test after you uncovered the fraud, but Winne put the vampires on it and we got it done in no time. You like the Office, don't you?"

"I haven't seen it."

"What? It's a classic."

It was a classic. So classic it had aired years before I was born. The look of disappointment Fred shot me was rich, though. He'd only discovered the comedy programme when Tristan had recommended it to him.

"Elle, can we talk?" Liam asked. He hadn't taken the hint to leave me alone to wallow in my embarrassment. I'd kissed a coworker. Despite the counsellor's advice to talk to him, I just wanted to disappear into a hole and ignore the problem. Besides, we couldn't discuss it here. The employee handbook was clear that nonconsensual contact constituted harassment, and I'd kissed him. I couldn't do this now.

"I don't get a lot of time to watch TV." I carried on talking to Fred. That wasn't a lie. My work kept me busy. The Bathory Corporation expected their graduates to work hard, and long hours were the norm here. Plus I had my accountancy exams to study for and there was a lot to read if I wanted to keep to my schedule of three exams per sitting. Besides, if I did watch TV, I wanted to slouch on the sofa staring at *Celebrity Baker* or *Love Peninsula*, not ancient sitcoms set in Slough.

"I'll have to introduce you to the joys of it, then." I didn't like the sly smile that crept onto the vampire's face. "Where have they got you nowadays?"

"I'm in the Archives." Pride shone through my voice. I was enjoying it, and my database project was going well. Plus it was a lot safer than the fae realm, where I had almost died. Twice.

"No wonder you don't like humour if you're down with that stuffy lot–"

"Elle, please." Liam reached for my hand.

I took a breath. He was right. We needed to talk. I needed to apologise. "I'm sorry for–"

Precious barged into our conversation without worrying about it looking rude. "Come on, Elle. Got to go." She linked her arm through mine and tugged me away from the two men.

As Precious led us away, the vampire turned to consider the lift that led to the Archives. Liam stared after me with a considering look on his face, like I was a problem he could solve. The problem was that part of me wanted to be solved.

I didn't have time to worry about what either of them might do, because Precious shoved me into a meeting room and shut the door behind me.

"What are we doing here? What about lunch?" I patted my bag where my sandwiches waited. Abby and I had splashed out this week on a fresh baked tiger loaf and my mouth watered just thinking about the crusty bread which I'd spread with real butter before layering on crispy lettuce, mature cheddar cheese and a slice of ham. It might not sound like much, but to me, it was a luxury.

"You can eat after."

"After what?"

"Our training."

Chapter 17

Orcs value toughness above all else. They train almost as soon as they take their first steps. A strong individual means a strong clan.

Slay Bloodbringer – *An Insight into Orc Behaviour*

I didn't have time to ask what she meant. Precious grabbed my arm and with a quick twist of her hips, threw me onto the carpeted floor. My head missed the leg of a chair by five millimetres.

"Your reactions are slow," said Precious, standing back and crossing her arms.

I rubbed my back. I had landed on my laptop bag in an awkward heap, and it dug into me. At least I'd left my laptop down in the Archives. I did not want to endure an awkward trip to IT and have to deal with Liam after I'd made an idiot of myself. No, it was only my sandwiches in danger of getting squashed.

With a shrug, I took off the bag and put it to one side. I knew I wouldn't get my lunch until Precious decided we were done.

"What do you expect? I don't know any martial arts. I'm a mathematician, not a fighter."

"You can be both."

I raised an eyebrow at her.

Precious reconsidered. "You can learn to defend yourself."

I considered telling her to get stuffed, but I didn't know how to defend myself. The horror of Albert's attack at the Christmas party rushed to the front of my mind. I had got away through luck and a kick to his crotch, not through any skill. If I closed my eyes, I could still see his leering face as he strangled me. His face dissolved, replaced by the vampire who'd attacked me at Blud last year and finally the bloke who'd got handsy last week. I took a shaky breath. I had to do this.

Precious placed a hand on my shoulder. "I can help."

"I don't want to feel helpless." I opened my eyes and looked into her guileless gaze. If she wanted to help me, I couldn't have a better teacher.

"You won't. I swear it." Precious held out her hand and closed her fingers over my wrist. I mirrored her. It felt like a warrior's oath.

Then she flexed her wrist and pain shot through my arm. I let out a yelp.

"There's no soundproofing in here," she said, releasing me

and stepping back.

"Don't scream. Got it. When do I get to use your knife again?"

She gave me a smile that made me shrink back and shrugged off her suit jacket. "When you earn it."

For the next forty-five minutes, Precious tried to teach me self-defence. All I learned was that she could hit hard, even when she pulled her punches. I almost got the hang of a tricky move to break out of someone's grip; you had to go limp so they thought you gave up and got lulled into a false sense of security before ducking down and back, pulling their body off balance so you could twist free. I had the going limp part down, but the twisting free ended with me colliding with the table Precious had moved to one side.

Tristan walked in during one attempt where I had managed to pull Precious on top of me. All six feet of her crushing my body into the carpet. He arched an eyebrow and leered at us. "Ladies, what's going on here?"

I tried to push Precious off. And failed.

"Use your hips," she said. "They're stronger than your arms."

I bucked against her. Tristan almost choked.

With a snort of frustration, Precious checked the time. "We're done here."

"No, no," Tristan said, "don't stop on my account. Things were just getting interesting."

Precious pushed herself up with ease and offered me her hand. She pulled me up with a strength I envied. "What do you want?" she asked Tristan as she bent to retrieve her lunch.

He eyed her bottom as her trousers stretched tight over it. "I missed you at lunch, then I saw you had this meeting room booked and thought I'd come say hi. I didn't know you two were getting down in here though, bit risky, isn't it? At lunchtime? In a meeting room right off the atrium?"

"We weren't–" I started.

"You're jealous," Precious said, taking a bite out of her homemade pasty.

"Jealous?" Tristan sputtered.

"Lonely, then."

"Maybe I want to be the one between your thighs," he said, placing an arm on the table and leaning forward.

Precious looked him up and down. "You couldn't handle me."

I snorted out a laugh and took a seat.

Tristan ignored me, his gaze fixed on Precious. "How about you try me out and we'll see what I can handle?"

I blushed as the tension in the room rocketed. Precious licked her lips and their gazes locked onto each other with a strange intensity that made me think I should go.

Then Precious shrugged, breaking the spell. "I'm eating my lunch."

Tristan reached out to her, maybe to stroke her hair, maybe

to pat her cheek. I never knew because Precious' hand moved fast as lightning, grabbing his pale hand in hers. She twisted it and Tristan fell off his chair with a howl of pain.

"You don't touch me without my permission."

"Alright, alright, sorry," Tristan gulped between sharp breaths. "Please, let me go."

Precious nodded and released him. "Because you said please." She turned to me. "You did alright."

"Really?"

"No. But you'll get better."

With that encouragement, I finally retrieved my sandwich to see that I had crushed the fluffy bread when I'd landed on my bag. It was as squashed as my confidence and the limp sandwich was as disappointing as the realisation that I had Kylie's workshop to attend this afternoon.

Chapter 18

Workshops are an important tool to test ideas and gather opinions. We encourage these at the Bathory Corporation.

Elizabeth Bathory – *The First Disrupter*

I limped up to the meeting room on the third floor behind Precious and Tristan who bickered about self-defence versus assault. I didn't have the energy to join in; I was too busy wondering how much I stank after the unexpected lunchtime exercise, and my dry-clean only suit dress was now covered with creases and carpet fluff. I had to stop buying dry-clean only clothes.

As we entered the room, Kylie looked up from where she was arranging coloured card on the tables laid out in a square horseshoe shape. She nodded. "Good, you're on time. Spread out, will you? There's more people coming and it'll look less intimidating if all the graduates aren't together."

Precious tipped her head to one side and sank into a chair

with a look that said she'd sit wherever she darn well pleased – although she wouldn't have said 'darn'. Tristan picked a spot opposite her with a wink.

I hesitated, torn between wanting to sit next to my friend and not annoying Kylie.

"Sit wherever you want, Elle," said Precious, hooking her foot around the chair next to her and pushing it out for me.

I lowered my head to avoid Kylie's gaze and sat next to her. "Is it normal to feel like my shoulder wants to separate from the rest of my body?" I whispered as I took out my notebook; a leatherbound number with a brass latch. I liked to match my notebooks to the occasion, and this had screamed Archives when I'd found it online doing some sad shopping during my lonely Christmas break. It was a present to myself.

"That means it was a good session. We'll meet twice a week until you can throw me off."

I gulped and poured myself a glass of water from the jugs Kylie had just placed in front of us. More people trickled in. Most of them sported bored expressions that said they thought this was a huge waste of time, but they couldn't get out of it. I recognised Edwyn from my first placement and gave him a nod.

He sat next to me. "How's it going?"

I startled. He had never been this nice to me. "Good. I'm in the Archives now."

Edwyn pulled a face. "I heard."

"No, it's alright. I'm building them a database."

He gave me a considered look. "Good for you."

"I heard you got the promotion you wanted."

A small smile tugged at his lips. "I did. Of course, thanks to your discovery, the Fae Audit department has lost some of its trust, so I've got two accountants on secondment reviewing old audits that Albert handled. We can't risk the company's reputation sinking any lower with our clients."

I gave him a weak smile in return. It wasn't my fault the previous audit director had teamed up with a fae to commit fraud. I'd just exposed it.

Kylie placed herself in front of the screen at the open end of the semi-circle of tables and coughed. When that didn't quiet the room, she looked around for something to tap against her glass of water. There were no convenient spoons, so she chinked two glasses together, spilling water all down her hands.

I felt a tug of sympathy as she swallowed before forcing a smile back onto her face.

"Thanks for coming to this mandatory workshop, everyone." There were a few grunts from some of us. I gave her an encouraging smile, knowing how it felt to be nervous and out of your depth. "We're here today to think about how we name the different areas of the company." She met everyone's gaze. Bless her, she was really trying to be engaging and change her image. Maybe she was more of a role model than I'd thought.

"You want us to change our department names?" asked

Edwyn, leaning back in his chair with a frown.

"Ah," said Kylie, lifting one finger. "That's the point. The Human Resources – I mean, People – team, thinks that 'department' is too divisive. It literally means 'a division in a company' from the Latin dispertire; 'to divide'. It's not the sort of joined up thinking we want at the Bathory Corporation, it's not promoting the right spirit."

"What is the right spirit for a company run by vampires?" someone asked.

"That's what we're here today to find out," Kylie said, unphased by the interruption. "We've come up with some alternatives that we want your opinions on. And other suggestions are very welcome, of course." She said the last sentence with a tone that suggested other options were not welcome at all.

"I'll put some words on the screen, and you give me your reactions. You can write them down if you want."

"Why is the card coloured?" asked Edwyn, holding up a pink A4 sheet.

"We're not at primary school," said Precious.

"I like it." Tristan selected a sunshine yellow piece of card.

Kylie's forced smile was back. "Colours promote creativity."

I raised an eyebrow at that and couldn't help looking around the grey-walled room. The card was the only thing in here not grey, white or black, if you didn't include Tristan's tie or Precious' green skin.

Kylie clapped her hands together. "Everyone ready to begin? Good. Here's the first word."

Community flashed up on the screen in a lime green font.

"Ugh," Edwyn grimaced, "it's a bit forced, isn't it?"

"Great feedback, write it down." Kylie pushed a piece of card towards him.

"I like it, fosters a sense of togetherness," said Tristan.

"Exactly," Kylie said. "That's the spirit."

I looked at Precious' card and snorted when I saw she'd written: This is ridiculous. I turned my snort into a cough when Kylie looked my way.

"Next word is 'clan'."

Precious shoved her chair back. "You can't use that."

"No? We thought it promoted belonging, inclusion–"

"It does, but it's more than that. It's knowing where you belong, it's like home but – there isn't a good word for it in English – it's knowing where you don't belong. It's an orc word." That was the most I'd ever heard Precious say in one go. "Use coven, that's the vampire term."

Tristan half-raised his hand. "I think coven is for witches."

Precious glared at him.

"He's right. Vampires have nests, but I've never liked that word. We don't usually go in for working together." The woman who spoke smiled and flashed her fangs. Her eyes glowed red. The tension that thrummed from Precious disappeared.

Edwyn shuddered. "Emotional vampire," he whispered to me.

The vampire heard. "And the anger in here is delicious." She flicked out her tongue and licked her lips.

"Wraith," Edwyn raised his voice, holding the vampire's gaze. "One who feeds on negative emotions."

The vampire grinned. "And I can feel your fear."

Kylie clapped her hands. "No feeding without consent. You know that, Raquel."

"My apologies, but her seething wrath is so tempting." Raquel fixed her gaze on Precious. "If you ever want to lose some of that anger, come see me. I'm up on sixth."

Precious pursed her lips and shook her head.

"Back to the matter at hand, I've noted orc connotations with 'clan'. We don't want to offend any sub-groups."

Precious stood and slammed a fist onto the table. "We are not a sub-group." With that, she grabbed her oversized handbag and stalked out.

Raquel beamed as she feasted on the new wave of emotion.

Kylie's smile became more strained. "Let's move to the next word."

My opportunity to follow Precious out had gone. I stared up at the flashing 'collective' on the screen and wrote down 'Borg' on my cardboard before crossing it out.

The rest of the afternoon passed in a blur of synonyms until the words whirled around my mind, losing all meaning:

neighbourhood, tribe, team, squad.

Kylie called it at half past five when even the emotional vampire looked drained. I considered going down to the Archives – I'd barely got any actual work done today – when Abby's text came through asking me if I was still on for tonight.

Drat. I was going to be late.

Chapter 19

Dear Abby, my friend is always late for anything we try to do together. I love her, but sometimes I feel like I don't matter, and it really bugs me. What should I do?

Honey, let's thought cake this. You love your friend, you told me so, that's a great foundation layer that any good sponge cake needs. But you feel like it's disrespectful – bam – we've got straight to the gooey centre of your problem. And I think you know what you need to do; talk to your friend. Explain how you feel, see if she can make an effort. And, if that fails, give her a fake time half an hour earlier than you need to meet. She'll end up being on time, then.

Cakefully yours, Abby

Abby Wright – *Ask Abby*

"**S**orry, sorry," I mumbled as I ran through our front door. "Do I have time to get changed?"

Abby checked her phone. "Five minutes."

I stumbled into my bedroom and peeled off my crumpled suit dress. I had the world's fastest shower because I hadn't had a chance after my lunchtime workout. I scrubbed myself with the strawberry milkshake body wash I had stocked up on in case the store ever discontinued the product, dried myself and changed into my fluffiest tartan pyjamas. They were hideous but obligatory for our comfort evening in. It was a relic of our time at university together; one evening a week to lounge about in our tiny student flat and watch bad TV while eating takeaway.

We both had jobs now, but little had changed except the location of our flat and the fact that I worked late so often now that we usually did this at weekends. But today was the start of the new season of *Love Peninsula* and Ahmed was a lot more relaxed about staying late than my previous team.

I topped up Nibbles' food and water and opened up his deluxe cage. He clambered out and made his way to the sofa where I lifted my guinea-pig sized hamster up to sit on the threadbare cushion. I know it sounds strange, but the little guy loved to watch TV with us, especially *Love Peninsula*. *Celebrity Baker* he could take or leave.

"So, did you talk to Liam?" Abby asked as she arranged the snacks on the table and started opening takeaway cartons.

"No." I reached for the box of spring rolls. Only one sat in there. That was ridiculous. I checked the menu. It definitely said there should be two in a portion. Great. "They've messed up our order."

"Do you want me to complain?" Abby asked.

"No," I sighed. I cut the roll in two and stared at it, trying to decide which was larger so I could give Abby the bigger portion.

She interrupted my indecision by stabbing the nearest half with her chopsticks. "Why didn't you talk to him?"

My brain was still stuck on the incorrect spring roll portion. "Who?"

"Liam."

"Oh. I couldn't. What if he doesn't like me? What if he thinks I assaulted him?"

Abby snorted. "He was probably happy you snogged him."

"It was hardly a snog."

"Talk to him."

"I will. Now," I changed the topic. "What do you think about Brian's chances with Candice?"

"I don't know. Cons; he's called Brian."

"You can't hold someone's name against them," I pointed out.

"Pros, he's got that brooding thing going for him."

"And Candice?"

"She's going to play hard to get, make him work for it, but they could be the couple of the season."

Chapter 20

Jelly is comprised of gelatine and water, usually with sugar and flavouring to make a sweet dessert; a perennial favourite of children's birthday parties and easy to make, although it takes time to set properly so is best prepared the night before.

Delilah Sweetling – *Celebrity Baker Popular Party Treats*

I walked into the office with a spring in my step. Our slouchy evening had rejuvenated me, and I was ready to build my database and deal with whatever the Bathory Corporation had to throw at me. And talk to Liam, if I could gather my courage.

"Morning Ahmed," I sang as I exited the lift.

A fruity citrus scent wafted over the reception area, covering the usual musty smell of old books and dust; the cleaners must have been down here.

Ahmed didn't reply. Probably enjoying a lie in. I walked over to the desk and let myself through. The cobweb feeling as I lifted the hinged hatch in the desk now felt natural.

The book display wheel held a new manuscript on it. I grinned. George had started leaving medieval scripts with interesting illuminated letters or marginalia – little drawings around the main text of a manuscript – out for me. I pored over the page, searching for whatever had piqued their interest and soon found what had caught their eye; women picking phalluses – or should that be phalli? – from a tree full of the things. Not work appropriate, but these medieval monks had some strange ideas.

Shaking my head, my gaze slid to Ahmed's inkwell. I hope my boss hadn't caught me smirking at inappropriate drawings, although maybe these were so old they counted as art…I froze.

Ahmed's inkwell was surrounded by green jelly. I moved closer and sniffed; lime flavour. That explained the sweet smell.

My mouth widened with horror. "Ahmed, can you hear me?" I prodded the jelly. It wobbled. There was no answer from inside the inkwell.

Had he put himself in a jelly bath? Possible, but he hadn't mentioned it, and wouldn't he reply? Did djinn – I'd looked up the plural online to better educate myself about the supernaturals I worked with – take jelly baths?

"Ahmed…the magnificent?" Something was off. Even if he told me to leave him alone, he'd say something. I'd never known Ahmed to ignore me before. Try to get me to read from a cursed book, sure, but he was polite and wouldn't leave me here calling for him.

So, the logical conclusion was that someone had put his inkwell in the jelly. Someone with access to the company who could leave it here to set overnight. A connection snapped in my brain. Someone who raved about an office-based programme that had a prank involving jelly…"Oh, Fred."

The doors to the lift slid open and a small fae stepped out. She had flowers in her hair and her brown skin shimmered like dew. Pytha. Another, taller fae with skin that feathered like silver birch bark followed her, his eyes darting around taking everything in.

"Good morning," Pytha said with a predatory grin. "You owe me a favour."

I swallowed. It was true. She had got a favour out of me in thanks for sending me through a portal in my first placement. "What do you want?" I crossed my arms. I wouldn't be so naïve this time, she wouldn't get any more favours from me.

Pytha tapped a long finger to her cheek. "How about a caramel macchiato from the place down the street?"

I knew where she meant. The Goblin Roast coffee shop nearby was legendary both for their delicious blends and their expensive prices.

"OK." A coffee was less than I expected for a favour.

"And you can answer this one's questions."

I narrowed my eyes and crossed my arms over my chest. "That's two favours."

"Worth a try. Fine," she huffed, "I'll go without the coffee. Answer his questions and your favour to me is complete." Pytha turned to the other fae. "And my favour to you is now paid."

He bowed and gave her a toothy smile.

Pytha turned on her delicate heels and flounced back to the lift.

"My questions," he started.

I held up a hand, surprised at my daring. "I'm in the middle of a situation here." I lifted the plate of jelly so he could see.

The fae's eyebrows shot up. "What is that…substance?"

"Jelly."

"Djeli?"

Close enough.

"Why is there an inkwell in there?" he asked, his lip curling as if this was some obscure human custom.

"That inkwell contains the djinni who runs this department," I said, tilting the plate as I examined it.

"And he likes being in djeli?" The fae leaned forward and sniffed. "Is it…food?"

"Haven't you had jelly before?" It was a staple at kids' birthday parties, but maybe the fae didn't celebrate birthdays.

"No."

"Let's get him out and ask him." It looked like ordinary jelly.

I put the plate back on the desk and flexed my fingers,

knowing that I would hate the feel of the goopy, slimy substance on my hands. But it had to be done. I couldn't leave in him there. Grimacing, I plunged one hand into the jelly. My fingers brushed the slippery surface of the glass inkwell, and I cleared the stopper, pulling globs of the substance off my boss's container.

As soon as the layer of jelly over the glass stopper was clear, Ahmed exploded out of the inkwell, sending the remaining fragments of jelly flying across the room. Some of it landed on me and I screwed up my face at the lime assault. He gasped a breath as though he'd been suffocating.

"You!" His voice boomed and he pointed a shaky finger at me. Ahmed puffed up into his full djinni form, dangerous and enormous, his black hair scraping the ceiling, his draping moustache trembling in anger. Dark storm clouds gathered around him, and the air crackled with static potential.

I backed away.

Ahmed's eyes glowed a dangerous gold, sparks bursting from them. "You trapped me!" The tip of his finger lit up with magic and he cast a bolt of lightning towards me.

Chapter 21

Workplace humour can be a strong bonding experience, but we encourage professionalism at all times.

Elizabeth Bathory – *The First Disrupter*

My body moved of its own accord, not wanting to be fried by an irate djinni. The lightning bolt passed overhead as I huddled in a small ball on the floor, my hands cradling my head. The tang of singed wood filled the air.

"Why would you trap me, Elle of the graduate scheme? I thought we were friends." Ahmed's voice still held the booming echoes of power, but now a trace of pain and betrayal lanced through it.

"We are. I didn't," I squeaked.

"You didn't?" Ahmed lowered himself from where he swirled near the ceiling and took his more human form, bending so he could peer at me where I cowered under the desk.

I blinked up at him, my face wet with tears, and shook my head. "I got you out."

"Then you rescued me. Thank you." Ahmed pulled me into a bear hug that rivalled George's squeezes and forced another squeak from me.

When he set me down, I trembled from shock. Ahmed clapped my shoulder, making me step forward from the force.

Over my head, he caught sight of the fae who watched us with a tilted head and a confused expression.

Ahmed puffed himself up. "So you are my tormentor." The djinni aimed his forefinger at the fae.

I placed my hand on his arm. "No, Pytha brought him. I have to answer his questions to fulfil my favour to her."

"Does the type of djeli matter?" the fae asked, using a long finger to wipe a smear of green from his cheek. He sniffed it with curiosity before sticking out his tongue and licking it. His mouth curdled into a sneer. "This is food?" he asked again.

Ahmed lowered his hand. "Djeli." He spat the word and glared at the lime globules that coated the desk, the walls, the ceiling, me and the fae. Muttering in a language I didn't understand, Ahmed snapped his fingers and all the fragments of jelly congealed back onto the plate, which now sat apart from his inkwell. He took a deep breath and when he turned back, a glassy smile curved his lips. "Enough of this silliness, how can we help a friend of Pytha's?"

The fae coughed and looked at us. "I have come to enquire about the precautions surrounding the Crown of Winter. It is a valuable fae artefact, as I'm sure the emperor told you."

"Oh, you work for him?" I asked.

"I have come to check how well you have guarded the crown."

"You don't have to worry," I said with a smile. Ahmed still looked like he was cooking up ways to kill whoever had covered his home with jelly. "We've taken every precaution. It's stored in the most secure section of the Archives; the restricted section."

"I take it there are wards." The fae sounded bored, but his eyes were bright and interested.

I nodded, keen to impress Ahmed with my understanding of our storage. "There are more wards around the section, as well as alarms and it is in the deepest part of the labyrinth."

"When was the last successful break-in to this place?"

Ahmed pulled himself away from whatever dark revenge he was plotting and eyed the fae. "There has never been anyone who made it past our wards who did not work here. You can be assured we are taking every precaution and please tell the emperor that if he has any concerns, he should come to me himself."

"I will report back," said the fae with a half bow.

"Is that it?" I asked. "Have I answered all your questions?"

The fae turned his back on me, then whirled back and held

up his finger, a number of emotions flickering across his face. "Where can I find more of this djeli?" His tongue sounded like it stuck on the word.

I frowned at him. Did he like the stuff that much after one taste? "Any supermarket should sell it. It's just jelly."

He nodded and this time he did leave. As the lift doors closed behind him, I sagged with relief, my promise to Pytha fulfilled and no longer hanging over me. I hadn't realised how much it weighed in the back of my mind until it was gone, and I felt freer, like I had more space in my brain to think.

Ahmed stopped glowering at the plate of messy goop that had been his prison and pursed his lips at me. "You must be careful with the fae, Elle. They cannot lie but they always have reasons upon reasons for anything they say. Do not offer up more than you have to."

I swallowed. So, I hadn't impressed Ahmed with my knowledge of the Archives, I had annoyed him by saying too much.

He patted my shoulder. "It is good you do not know how the wards are cast or you might have given him some useful information."

"Oh, right." I shuffled my feet. Ahmed stayed silent, waiting for me to ask. "How did jelly stop you from getting out from your inkwell?"

The djinni's brow crinkled. "I am not sure. I have been thrown in oceans and been able to escape, but this…it was like being buried. When there is sufficient pressure on the lid,

I cannot get out."

"So someone can hold you in?"

He shook his head. "No, merely pressing on the stopper would not prevent me from getting out. It is an enigma how this…jelly as you call it," again, he spat the word, "prevented me from leaving my abode. Who would even do this?"

"Er…"

Ahmed whirled to face me. "What do you know?" The booming echo of power was back in his voice.

"I think it was a prank," I whispered.

"A prank? A joke! I was trapped in there! A prisoner in my own home! For a joke?!"

"It's from a programme called the Office, there's a stapler in some jelly, I think." I'd never actually watched the TV series, just seen clips.

"I am not a stapler!"

"I know."

Ahmed narrowed his eyes. "Oh, but if someone thinks they can be pranking me then I will show them that I am the master of the jokes." He rubbed his hands together in a sinister way that reminded me of a Disney villain.

Now that he had a new purpose, Ahmed relaxed back into the boss I knew and I twirled a piece of hair between my fingers, considering if I could ask him a question I'd been mulling.

"What is it, Elle? I can feel you thinking."

I swallowed. Now or never. "Why is your home an inkwell?"

"Would you rather I lived in a lamp?" Ahmed's voice flattened so I knew I was on dangerous ground.

"I mean, why here? At the Bathory Corporation?"

Ahmed sighed and conjured up a chair to sink into. "It is hard to find peace in this world. There are always people who want to capture me and use my power for their own ends. Elizabeth found my inkwell in an antique shop. When she found the true extent of the bottle's secrets and released me, I was resigned to yet another term of servitude. But, instead, she set me free, then offered me a contract." He stared into space, his eyes focused on some point in the distant past.

"Wow," I breathed. I already idolised the woman, but hearing about Elizabeth Bathory's supernatural philanthropy took my admiration to new heights. "So that's why you work here. At the Bathory Corporation, I mean, to pay back that debt."

"Hmmm?"

"You're a master of the magical arts and served kings and queens. Why else do you protect the Archives down here in the basement?"

"Ah, to be so young and see things in black and white." He sighed and stayed silent for so long that I thought he wouldn't answer me. But then he spoke, his deep voice echoing in the empty vault. "I work for them because I can. Because I have a choice."

I frowned.

"The life of a djinni is one of servitude. I am a powerful spirit, but I was captured by a sorcerer, forced to carry out their bidding. When that term ended, he passed my container – a lamp, of all things, could it be any more cliché? – to his apprentice and so on for a long line. Once in a while, I received a new container as fashions changed, but never free. There used to be a good trade in djinn, we were seen as little more than slaves you did not have to feed or clothe, and we work miracles with the merest click of our fingers. How do you think the pyramids and other wonders were built?

"But freedom, the choice to work or not to work, it is a thing of rare wonder for me. And that, young Elle, is why I choose to work here. Not because I have to, but because I can. And in exchange, I receive the same benefits as anyone else. And that is important."

Chapter 22

Persistence is the key to solving most problems.

Elizabeth Bathory – *The First Disrupter*

I didn't know how to respond to Ahmed's revelation, and he didn't seem to want to talk anymore, so I flicked open my laptop and got on with my database project while he polished his inkwell, muttering about revenge and jelly.

With no funding, I had to use a basic version that came with the laptop, and I was testing it on the nearest portions of the Archives before venturing deeper into the stacks. My process was simple; select an item stored here, note its reference and location codes in my database along with a description and I'd set up tags for things like magic or how it was stored.

The problem was that I didn't really know much about anything stored here. Books seemed the most obvious thing to start with because they at least had titles inscribed on their spines or in their pages, and Ahmed trusted me to handle them if I wore protective gloves that made my fingers itch but meant any oils on my skin didn't damage the precious tomes.

However, not all the books were in English and, while I could copy down anything in the alphabet even if the words didn't make sense, I couldn't do the same for anything in Greek or Arabic or Cyrillic, let alone some of the Hieroglyphs I came across.

My next experiment involved taking pictures with my laptop camera, but the quality was so poor in the atmospheric lighting that I might as well have not bothered with that. I turned to a new page in my Archives notebook – the leather one with the brass clasp – to ask Ahmed if I could use my phone if I promised to delete the pictures once I'd emailed them to my work address.

He agreed but drew the line at using flash photography in case it upset the artefacts or the dragon. So now I had pictures, which were a little better but not perfect.

I rotated the display wheel past another manuscript open on a page where a centaur played a trumpet while a face on his bottom stared at some fruit – where had George found that? – until the large catalogue faced me. Ahmed had disappeared, possibly back into his newly cleaned inkwell, so I approached the humongous book by myself. I opened it to the first page, wrinkling my nose at the musty smell of old pages and dust, and ran my gloved finger down the column of faded spidery writing. Even though I squinted and tried both standing back and leaning closer, I couldn't make out anything beyond the odd word.

I gave a grunt of frustration before shutting the book and hefting it onto its front cover; if I started at the back, with the newer entries, maybe I could read the entries at least. My idea worked. Sort of. It was indeed easier to read the fresher writing; the very last entry was the Crown of Winter written in a clear hand in black ink next to the name of the fae emperor and an entry number.

I copied the information onto my laptop. But, what I couldn't do going this way, was check whether the items were in the location the catalogue proclaimed, or even check if they were in the Archives at all. I had helped George store the crown, but I wasn't wandering the corridors by myself to find items that may or may not be there. I knew in my bones that my database idea was good, but there were so many hurdles in my way and I worried I didn't have enough time or knowledge to do a good job, and that was what I wanted to do, what I had to do.

Even if I didn't want a long-term career in the Archives, I did want a decent performance review and I needed to impress Ahmed and George. Hard work and impressing people was my path to becoming the youngest director in Bathory Corporation history. It was all I wanted to do. And I felt like I was failing.

"All I want to know is whether the entry for the Canterbury Tales matches the one I found," I said in frustration, naming one of the books I could read the title of.

The catalogue shivered under my fingers, and I stepped back, my gaze darting around the office. What had I done? An idea took hold. If Ahmed had made the catalogue magical… but if it was, then I didn't want to be anywhere near it if my idea failed. I backed away until I was as far as possible from the book and risked saying 'Canterbury Tales' again.

The catalogue pages flipped with a sudden speed until the book lay open. I moved closer, still looking around guiltily. Squinting at the columns of entries, I recognised the title and did a whoop of joy. I didn't understand how the catalogue worked, but I'd take any help I could get.

I cross-referenced the written entry with my database and confirmed the match with a tick in the catalogue column before adding a fresh column to record the page number of the catalogue. That would help with any future searching, and whoever maintained the database after me wouldn't have to worry about whether the catalogue was magic or not, they could simply turn to the correct page.

I scanned the next row in my database, wondering if I could ask the catalogue again and if it would respond the same way – maybe the Canterbury Tales had been a fluke? – and the glimmer of hope fluttering in my chest winked out.

I didn't even know what the next artefact was called, and 'gold ring with red stone' wasn't specific enough to help. I tried anyway, more out of desperation then expectation and the catalogue stayed still. Backing up to give it space to work its magic, I balanced the laptop on my forearm and repeated the description from across the room. The catalogue gave the bookish equivalent of a shrug and the pages stayed still. So either it had been a fluke or I hadn't given the catalogue enough information.

On a whim, I read out the reference number. Each artefact stored in the Archives had one, and a location code, and the ring's had been scrawled on a sturdy cardboard tag attached to it with a small length of standard string.

The pages fluttered and I let out a squeak of excitement. It worked! I ran forward, and my laptop fell from my shaky grasp onto the floor. I swore. Darn it. I had been so close. Bending down, I picked up the laptop. A large crack spread across the screen, bisecting it into unequal halves. Behind the crack, I could make out my database. Maybe that meant that the hard drive was intact. Mentally crossing my fingers, I rested the laptop on the desk and hurried to the book.

I didn't want to lose my chance at getting data from the book while it worked, so I took out my notebook, resorting to analogue record keeping to write down all the information I could make out on the ring. It had been stored back in the fifties, so the entry was relatively fresh compared to the artefacts noted at the start of the catalogue. I scribbled down the reference number and all the other details I could see before tucking my notebook away and retrieving my laptop. I'd update the entry it in my database later, once my laptop was fixed.

My body tensed, and my stomach coiled with embarrassment. I couldn't avoid Liam any longer. Time to go visit the IT department and have a Talk.

Chapter 23

Where possible, it is more cost effective to repair laptops than to replace.

Bathory Corporation IT policy (hardware)

The IT department was also situated on the lower floors, but not quite as deep underground as the Archives, just one floor below the executive suite. And if you're wondering why the executives weren't all lording it above us on the top floor like in other companies, then maybe you've forgotten that the Bathory Corporation is run by vampires who don't typically enjoy sunlight streaming through glass-panelled walls.

Anyway, I didn't have to go to the executive suite, I was headed to IT. The corridors on the IT floor were a dingy grey that sapped my energy as I made my way to the computer room.

Could the entire building be some sort of vampire, leeching

out emotions like that woman in the workshop? I peered through the small glass window on the door, hoping to catch someone's eye, but all I could see were dismembered laptops and rows of dark screens.

I rapped my knuckles against the door, balancing my still open laptop on one arm. No one answered. Maybe the department had been called away to some IT emergency. I almost wanted that to be the case, so I didn't have to deal with seeing Liam again and explaining that the kiss meant nothing – except it might, and that was why I had avoided him. I bit my lip as I considered what to do, but the practicality of not being able to do any work with a cracked screen lent me the courage to try the door. I was a professional archivist, dammit – sort of – and I would not be cowed by a door.

It opened, which I wasn't expecting. I edged inside and looked around properly. It looked like the room where computers came to die. The walls were the same depressing shade of grey as the corridors, only somehow worse. There were no windows – no point this far underground – and the walls were lined with metal shelving that housed rows of laptops, some with obvious parts missing. A red phone hung on one wall, presumably for emergency IT calls.

In the corner, Liam sat hunched over some circuit boards with his wireless headphones on. He paused whatever he was doing to drum a beat onto the desk before kicking his swivel chair round. He stuck out his lower lip and bobbed his head in time to whatever music he had pounding through his headphones. As he saw me, his face creased into surprise and he yanked his headphones off, sending his glasses tumbling to the floor.

"Elle!" He bent to retrieve his glasses before blinking up at me.

I grinned at him, my stupid face reacting on its own.

"How long have you been there?" He meant 'how much had I seen'. Guess I wasn't the only one embarrassed today.

"Long enough," I said.

He huffed a sigh and raked a hand through his headphone-flattened hair.

I gave him a break. Who was I to judge what got him through the day when I enjoyed a sudoku or a maths problem in the evenings when I wasn't studying or watching reality TV with my flatmate? "At least I didn't catch you watching porn." I regretted the words as soon as they were out of my mouth. It wasn't playful office banter, it was totally inappropriate.

Liam's cheeks reddened and mine overheated. But he recovered faster and said, "I haven't finished getting around the company firewalls yet."

I let out a relieved laugh. He wasn't going to report me to HR, I mean the People department, or clan, or whatever they were called.

"So, what brings you to my domain? Are the boxes in the Archives not depressing enough for you?" I was carrying a laptop, so it was pretty obvious why I'd ventured to IT, but I appreciated the attempt at small talk. And he hadn't asked why I'd avoided him, so I was grateful for that.

"Actually it's really interesting and I've got a project that I think I might have made a breakthrough on. But, I dropped my laptop." I held it out with both hands like it was an offering.

Liam sucked in a whistle. "That is a proper crack."

My heart fell. "Can you fix it?"

Liam's smile warmed me to the soles of my feet. "I can fix anything with a screen. Pass it over." He grabbed some cables from a drawer and connected my laptop up to a spare screen which lit up with my display. "Looks like everything's alright inside, but I'll run some diagnostics to be sure. Is there anything you want to save before I start? I might have to reboot it."

I pulled up one of the many swivel chairs that littered the room and rushed to save my database down, making sure I put it in a shared drive rather than saving it locally on my laptop. I did the same with my proposal; it was already saved in a shared drive, but I opened and resaved it just to be sure. Then I opened my emails to send myself the feedback file I'd started. Anytime someone gave me some feedback, I noted it down in a word document on the local drive, so I was more prepared when I needed to craft my performance review. I didn't want that on the shared drive, so an email would do.

As I pressed send, I noticed a companywide email from Kylie. I opened it and scanned through before groaning. She'd gone with Collective to replace department.

"What's the matter?" Liam kicked his chair to my side. His fingers brushed mine as he leaned forward to read the email, sending a jolt through my body. I pulled my hand away and placed it in my lap. "Typical," he said. "So we're the IT Collective now." He made a face. "It sounds like a bad Star Trek villain."

"That was my feedback."

We shared a smile. I might have giggled. "So, this has happened before?"

"They do something like this about every three years. Last time, they changed the company values so the acronym didn't spell BLOOD."

"What O did they lose?" I asked. Our company values of Bravery, Overachievement, Loyalty, and Drive spelled BOLD. You couldn't miss it; the values were on posters in hallways all over the building as well as painted in dark colours in the lobby.

Liam screwed up his face. "I think it was Organised? Or maybe Ornery?"

I giggled. "OK, I'm done with the laptop. Will it take long?"

He raised an eyebrow at me. "I'm going to run diagnostics and replace the screen. It might need a reboot. It'll be at least an hour."

I nodded, that wasn't too bad.

"But you're not first in the queue. I've got to sort some hardware for a batch of new starters for Monday."

"They're not even in the building yet," I protested, "can't you bump me up?"

A playful glint came into his brown eyes. "I mean, I could, but you're asking me to go against protocol here."

I hung my head. I didn't want to get him into trouble.

"What's it worth to you?" he asked.

I looked up at him through my eyelashes. Was he flirting with me? I bit my lower lip and considered what to say but nothing helpful came to me. "What's the going rate?" I asked, sounding too clinical, like I was getting a price for contents insurance.

Liam pretended to think for a moment before his gaze locked with mine. "How about a date?"

Chapter 24

Dear Abby, This guy I like asked me out, but I haven't had the best experiences with relationship and I haven't planned for love and I want to focus on my career. What should I do?

Honey, The guy you like asked you out - is this even a problem? But OK, let's thought cake it and dig into those layers. You thought you had one priority; work, so a relationship wasn't in your plans, that's the hard coating of royal icing around your heart. But if we scoop a little deeper, I think you do actually want love, otherwise you wouldn't write to me, you'd just turn him down and move on. So I think you have some work to do to move past your bad relationship experiences and figure out what your real priorities are, and – surprising, I know – there are lots of people who have both a career and a love life. I suggest you follow your heart.

Cakefully yours, Abby.

Abby Wright – *Ask Abby*

I froze. A date? The good news was that he felt something for me, and I might feel something for him too.

The con in the room was that I hadn't planned for any sort of relationship in my ten-year plan to become the youngest director in the company's history. I wasn't even convinced that a healthy relationship was possible; I'd seen unhealthy relationships too many times in the foster system. All falling in love ever got anyone was heartache and, worse, I'd seen people lose themselves, turn from confident overachievers to meek shadows as they got consumed by the relationship.

"We don't have to, if you don't like me." Liam's voice was a hoarse whisper in the dull IT room. "But when you kissed me…I thought you might want to, you know, see if there's chemistry."

"I'm thinking," I said, deciding on honesty. It always took time to work through complicated equations, and I liked Liam. That simple thought sent a wave of heat followed by a chill up through my body. I liked him. I hadn't planned to like anyone, but his awkward charm and friendly manner had worked through my defences and got hooks into my heart that pulsed electric whenever he was near.

"I don't want to ruin my career." I sounded callous, and the words rolled around in my mind like a hollow echo. I was in my second placement; I barely had a career. And yet one wrong move could destabilise everything. Or give me everything I never thought I could have. I was definitely overthinking this, but I could see so many paths spreading out before me that it paralysed me into indecision.

"Hey," Liam took my hand, "I'm not talking about the rest of our lives together. One date. That's all."

One date. I could do that. I nodded and squeaked out a "Yes." Abby was going to freak out when I told her.

Liam's grin lit up the room and there was a new bounce to his hands as he turned to my laptop.

"What should I do while you fix it?" I asked.

"I've got a few ideas," Liam said with a wink that made me blush beetroot red.

As I wondered if I'd made a terrible mistake, Liam's boss walked in and stretched. "I love helping out the consulting team, they've got so much energy, it's practically criminal. Oh, but who is this?" He looked down at me with a predatory smile.

"Liam's fixing my laptop," I said, feeling that I needed to explain my presence in the room.

"Is he now?" The man's gaze shifted to the workbench where Liam now hunched over my laptop, all his former positive vibes gone.

"I think you should go back to work. I'll bring your laptop down when it's done," he said in a curt voice that had no trace of flirting or even friendliness in it.

I nodded and fled the room. What had changed? We were getting on, I'd agreed to a date and then he'd closed down as soon as his boss walked in. My thoughts skittered back a step; I'd agreed to go on a date.

As the elevator doors opened to the Archives, I realised I couldn't work without my laptop, and I really wanted to call Abby. So, I grabbed my phone and hurried up to the lobby where I could make a call. I found a secluded bench facing out onto the courtyard garden at the back of the building and dialled Abby.

"Elle? What's wrong? Are you hurt?" Abby's worried voice came through my phone crystal clear.

"What? No. Nothing's wrong. Why would anything be wrong?"

"You called me," Abby said, as if that explained anything. As I stayed silent, trying to figure out what she meant, my friend sighed and said, "No one calls unless it's an emergency. That's why we have the chat app."

"Oh. Sorry to worry you. I just had something I wanted to talk to you about."

"Oooo, interesting. Spill," she ordered.

I swallowed and rushed out the words. "I'mgoingonadate."

"Pardon?"

"I've got a date," I said, more slowly, calming my racing heart which threatened to thud its way out of my chest as the excited terror of having a real date flooded me.

Abby squealed and shouted, "Yes! Finally!"

I looked around to make sure no one had heard her outburst.

"Who is he? She? Where are you going? I need details."

"*He* is Liam. He works in IT."

"Ooo," she said, "the hot guy from the club. I knew it when I saw you two together at Blud last year."

"He had a girlfriend back then."

"But he chose to make sure *you* were alright."

I chewed that over for a moment until Abby asked where we were going again.

"I don't know where we're going because I only just agreed. Should I have asked for more information? I should go back and ask."

"No!" Abby took a few breaths as if she needed to calm herself. "This is good. You can text him to ask and then we can plan."

"Oh. I don't have his number."

I could hear Abby putting her hand over her eyes. Dating was already complicated, and we hadn't even got to the going out part. "You work together, right? So email him your number, then he'll text you."

"What if he doesn't?"

"Elle," Abby said slowly as if explaining something to a child, "he asked you out. He likes you. He'll get in contact."

"OK."

"Stop freaking out. It's just a date. We'll strategize together when we know where you're going."

"Do we need a strategy?" That was the sort of thing you did for corporate planning. "We're not planning a merger."

"Oh Elle." Now I could feel Abby shaking her head. Relationships were complicated, and I wasn't even in one.

Fred, the vampire from Fae Audits caught my eye and gave me a wave before heading over.

"Got to go Abby," I said, keen not to be seen on a personal call during work time.

"Give him your number, stop freaking out and we'll talk tonight." Abby ended the call, leaving me to stew over her words as Fred sauntered over.

"So, how did it go?" he asked.

I looked at him blankly. How did he know about my love life?

"The jelly?" he prompted.

"Oh." Of course he was behind the prank. "I don't think Ahmed was a fan."

The vampire clamped his lips together as he sniggered before asking, "Was he a *trifle* upset?"

I grimaced at the poor pun. "No. He was incensed. That jelly trapped him in his inkwell for hours."

Fred shrugged. "I can't help it, I'm an evan-jelly-ist for the Office. Get it, like evangelist." He laughed at his own joke.

"No, I get it." It just wasn't funny.

"Tell that stick in the mud genie that he needs to get a sense of humour and I'm happy to help, any time." With that, he started an odd dance while making a weird noise that might have been a tune before putting his hands in his pockets and sauntering off, whistling the same almost tune as he shimmied across the lobby back to the Fae Audit Department.

Chapter 25

Unlike many others in this country, I believe in equality. All species are welcome and tolerated in our organisation, as long as they work hard.

Elizabeth Bathory – The First Disrupter

With no laptop, I decided to have a full hour for my lunch break, which meant I had time for a walk. It was a fine day – a rarity for the beginning of February – so I went to the local favourite coffee shop; Goblin Roast.

As I walked up, I saw a green-skinned goblin cleaning the wall with a sponge. Every so often, they would stop and wipe their nose. I got closer and saw they were scrubbing at graffiti. Most of the words were gone, but the picture was clear; a crude spray paint goblin strung up by a noose over a fire.

"I'm so sorry," I said as I walked up to them. I wrung my hands together, wanting to do something to help, even if it would mess up my work clothes.

"Just stupid kids," said the female goblin. Her lips trembled.

"Can I help?" I asked.

She shook her head, and her large, pointed ears wobbled. "Nothing to do but clean it off. Police are investigating. We have cameras."

"Are you open?" I wanted to hit myself. That was insensitive.

"Yes, we are open. It will take more than paint to close down the Goblin Roast café. Please, please," she bowed me inside.

An older goblin hovered behind the low counter, mopping at the pristine surface with a white cloth. He wiped at his eyes as I came in. "How can we be helping you? Special season promotion on blossom tea."

"Thanks. I'll take a hot chocolate." I couldn't understand people's obsession with tea and coffee, it was dirty, bitter water with a splash of milk, but hot chocolate…give me a creamy, rich hot chocolate any day of the week. I still wanted to do something to help the café so I asked for a deluxe and then ordered drinks for Ahmed, Dedomena and George, guessing at what they might enjoy, telling the goblin to keep the change.

"Sorry about outside," I said as the goblin made the drinks.

His eyes brimmed with tears. "My daughter is good girl, she don't want me to see. But I see. Was told this was good place to live, no fighting, not like home, but this is second time in month. I just want to grind beans, sell coffee, make living."

He shook his head. "Maybe it was stupid idea. Maybe should sell and do something else."

"You can't give up on your dream!"

He set the drinks on the counter and squinted up at me. "Dream is not more important than people, than family. When do stop being paint on walls and start being hurting family?" He sighed. "But, goblins is not so easy to get rid of." He gave me a small smile. "You see. Police can't stop, but goblins can stop."

I swallowed. That sounded like he was planning something illegal. I didn't know what goblins could do, but as he twisted a few loose paperclips into something that looked like a dagger, I was sure he could protect himself.

"I'll tell everyone at work to come," I said, gathering up my drinks.

He nodded and turned away. It was a stupid thing to say anyway, this was the go to coffee place for the Bathory Corporation, but maybe I could speak to Kylie and get HR – I mean, the People Collective – to say something about supporting a local business.

I slipped a note into the tip jar and headed to the office, unable to take my gaze from the disturbing picture on the wall.

Chapter 26

Persistence is the key to solving most problems.

Elizabeth Bathory – *The First Disrupter*

Back in the Archives after my decent lunch break at Goblin Roast, I found my laptop waiting for me with a sticky post-it note attached to the lid.

All sorted, I didn't have to reboot. Here's my number. Looking forward to our date, Liam x

I copied his number into my phone. Abby was right; he had made sure he got in contact. Now the ball was in my court, but I'd wait until I'd had time to strategize with Abby tonight before texting him. I had never had to deal with this sort of thing before and was likely to mess it up if I tried to go solo when I had a literal advice columnist at home. I sent her a picture of the note, and she replied with a thinking emoji. I guessed that meant we would chat later as she didn't send anything else.

Back in possession of my laptop, I felt like I could make real progress, but I wanted to check something in the data lake first. Ahmed was nowhere to be seen, and George was probably on their rounds. I called their name into the darkness of the labyrinth but heard no reply.

So, I did what any over-achieving graduate scheme member would do; I walked in alone.

Moving slowly, I checked my coordinates every three shelves or so and noted them down in my book. I also had an idea that the labyrinth liked intention, so I mumbled aloud that I wanted to find Dedomena in case that helped. More likely, it made me sound like a crazy person, but I was on my own in an endless labyrinth, so forgive me for wanting the company of my own voice.

I had the coordinates of the archway that led to her data lake in my notebook, and I was confident I was heading in the right direction, but it was still unsettling. The corridors stretched on in unending blackness either side of the dim lights that lit up above my head, keeping up with my progress through the passages and strange noises echoed through the empty corridors.

I'd accompanied George on enough rounds to keep my cool, but it was the sort of place where you expected a skeleton to jump out from behind a stack of artefacts.

I paused at a stack of medieval manuscripts. These looked like they might have those marginalia that George was so fond of…I selected one and paused, turning the very edge of the pages carefully until I found a giant letter M where a man vomiting made up part of the letter. George would love it.

I tucked it under my arm to put on the book display wheel later and kept going through the dim corridors.

Every so often, something on a shelf would rustle or thud causing me to jump and wonder if I should look closer or move faster. I plumped for moving faster. Who knew what protective measures or creatures lived here? I mean, George and Ahmed did, obviously, but there wasn't a list that anyone had shown me and my trip with George had only covered a tiny fraction of the Archives. The only thing I knew for sure lived in the labyrinth was George, Dedomena, a group of piskies and a dragon.

Chanting Dedomena's name, I moved forward, following twists and turns until…there! Her arch glinted under the next set of lights. I almost sobbed with relief. I'd found it. I'd entered the labyrinth and found what I was looking for. This placement would work out, the maze accepted me. And now I could check in and see if my database project was feasible.

I stepped through the arch with my back straight, clutching my newly repaired laptop to my chest. That sensation of cobwebs brushing against my skin hit me as I passed through, but it disappeared as soon as I entered the dazzling cavern.

The water sparkled and I moved closer before remembering

that it might ensorcel me. I took my earbuds out of my pocket and tucked them into my ears before finding a rock to set my laptop on. Spring moss covered the surface, but it was dry, so I loaded up my database and then called out to Dedomena.

The naiad's fronds broke through the still surface of the sparkling lake first and she rose up until she stood balancing upon the water like some Greek goddess, which I suppose she was, sort of. Strings of numbers zipped past just under the surface as data moved from one place to another in her data lake.

"Elle, the graduate." Dedomena peered past me. "Is George with you?"

I shook my head. "I wanted to ask you something."

The naiad arched an eyebrow and stepped closer, the water rippling with each step. I looked away as each time she moved, her barely-there clothing shifted over her plump curves. It never totally revealed her body but gave the promise of bare skin underneath. If that was what she chose to wear to work, no wonder the ancient Greeks found nymphs so attractive.

I shifted on the rock, my sensible heels no help in the uneven cavern.

"You are the first human in a long time to seek me out," she said, tipping her head to one side. "How may I help you?"

"I brought you a coffee." I had no idea if the lake nymph liked caffeine, but I figured it was better to offer something as tribute if she was some sort of minor deity. An expression I couldn't identify flickered across her face then was replaced by a beneficent smile. She reached out and took the coffee from me, sniffing at the paper cup.

I coughed. "Before I ask my questions, is there any price attached?" I had learned my lesson from working with Pytha and other fae, and I didn't want to get caught into some sort of favour exchange or bargain away part of my soul to ask some questions.

Dedomena laughed and the lake splashed in response. A couple of spreadsheets lapped at the edge of the water, snagged by the rocky side. I pointed and Dedomena shrugged and waved them back into the lake. "They were only month end reports and there were several errors in them. The accountant hasn't realised that a third of the formulas are broken and haven't updated in four months."

"Shouldn't you tell them?"

"It's not my role to point out errors, I store what I'm asked to store."

The thought of errors in our month end reports made me queasy and I asked for the names of the reports so I could say something.

Dedomena gave me a soft smile. "I cannot breach my privacy protocols. If you want that information, you would have to swim into the lake yourself."

I shuddered and wrapped my arms around myself. I couldn't swim. Not more than an awkward doggy paddle anyway and I didn't fancy risking my life to get some reports. I stared at the dark shapes swirling in the water and backed away from the lake – who knew what monsters lurked in there? I'd almost been killed by going for a swim in the fae lands, so no, I wasn't going into the naiad's lake by choice, but she'd mentioned accountants, so maybe I could tell someone in the Finance Department – sorry, Collective – and they could look into it. Filing that thought away in the back of my mind, I shook my head at Dedomena.

She shrugged as if it didn't matter one jot to her if I went into the lake or not. "What are your questions?"

"The price?" I replied, realising she still hadn't answered my earlier question.

Dedomena's lazy smile broadened. "There is no price. We both work for the same corporation, and your tribute of caffeine is sufficient."

I exhaled, grateful that someone in this organisation seemed to play fair. Sometimes it seemed like a cut-throat high school where everyone jostled for position and the vampires sucked everyone dry. I was grateful that I could hide from some of that down here in the coolness of the Archives with people who didn't seem likely to kill me on a whim.

"I've started creating a database for the Archives."

Dedomena stopped sipping her coffee and moved closer as I turned the laptop screen round so she could see what I'd done so far. I walked her through it, less of a sales pitch than I'd done with Ahmed and George, but more technical.

She tapped a long finger against her chin and then sat, cross-legged in front of the laptop, leaning forward. I averted my gaze from her gaping robes. "May I?" she asked.

I nodded and took my hands away from the keyboard. The naiad used the trackpad to navigate through what I'd done to date, noting the column names and the few sample artefacts I'd included so far.

"It's an interesting concept and one no one has tried before," she said, once she'd seen enough of my efforts.

"I was hoping I could sync it with your storage, unless it does that already? It's on the shared drive." I had no idea how the data lake worked and didn't want to annoy the deity with my ignorance of her world.

"You've got a simple object-oriented database. What's your interface?"

"Er…"

"So people can search it."

"I haven't got that far."

Dedomena squinted at the screen. "Is this built in Microsoft Access?"

"I don't have any budget, so I had to use the software on my laptop."

The naiad ran her hand down her face in a long-suffering motion. "Right, I'm giving you access to the SQL server so you can create the database in there." She pointed her hand at the laptop. When nothing happened, she tapped the side of the screen then asked me to stand back.

I retreated to near the entrance, touching the pads of my fingers to my thumb as I tried to ignore company rules about letting other people work on your laptop. But she was doing some sort of upgrade, which made her almost the IT department and they were the exception to that policy. That's what I told myself anyway as she thwacked the laptop, and it glowed a wet blue before the screen settled back to its usual colours.

"There. A little connection issue, but it's sorted now. I've copied in your database so far and added the standard company interface so anyone can use it." Dedomena caught the look on my face. "Don't worry, you're in a secure, separate part of the server so you can't mess anything else up by accident and I've linked access to Archive employee log-ons so no one else in the company can search it, for now. And I'll sort you out some R Fae ID cards; they'll work much better with the magic down here."

"I don't know any computer languages if this needs programming," I protested.

Dedomena cocked her head to one side and gave a me a smile that made me shudder like a chill mist was surrounding me. "Then you'd better learn."

With that, she turned and walked back into her data lake. The crystals lighting the grotto shone as bright as ever, but I got the message; our time was done.

Chapter 27

Many problems can be solved by making a simple list of pros and cons.

Elizabeth Bathory – *The First Disrupter*

Back at the flat and exhausted from trying to learn basic SQL all week so I could work with the new database format Dedomena had set up for me, I slumped onto the squashy sofa. It was old, worn down by many former bottoms, but it moulded to both me and Abby like we were part of it and after cleaning the apartment on rainy days, curled up with a blanket, there was nowhere I'd rather be.

It had taken a week for our schedules to align, but Abby and I had an evening together.

Nibbles squeaked from his cage, and I got up and passed a hamster treat through the bars. He hoovered it up, shoving the entire stick into his cheeks so they stuck out. I shook my head at the greedy hamster and let him out of his luxury cage.

"Do you think I should get him another run?" I mused out loud.

Abby snorted. "His maze already takes up half the wall, if you get him any more, we'll have to move the TV into the kitchen, and then where can I cook?"

Maybe she was right. I spoiled Nibbles and had created a snaking maze of plastic tubes that joined two cages with stopping points in between. But he'd been my one constant companion since I was thirteen when I'd found him wandering the streets.

My foster parents at the time had made me put up lost animal posters but no one had claimed him and I'd screamed and threatened to call the police when I overheard them talking about flushing him down the toilet, so they'd let me keep him with some provisos; he had to stay in my room, and I had to care for him with my own money.

So, I'd done what any thirteen-year-old would do; tutored my classmates for cash and sold my lunchtime chocolate bars at an inflated price until I had enough for a cage and food. When word spread about my maths knowledge, I started tutoring older kids too and that kept Nibbles in hamster treats right the way through school. He came with me every time I moved home, and I even smuggled him into student halls when I was at uni. Nibbles was my oldest friend, outliving the normal hamster lifespan several times over. But his enormous tube maze was in danger of taking over the living room.

I put him in his blue see-through plastic exercise ball; a custom-made model because he was a guinea-pig sized hamster. He chirruped and did a token lap around our tiny flat before ramming the ball against the sofa so hard the hatch popped open. Free from his spherical prison, he climbed up and made himself comfortable on the arm of the sofa before taking the treat out from his cheek pouch and nibbling on it.

"So, back to Liam," Abby said.

I groaned. We had dissected every conversation I could remember, and my head pounded from the strain of analysing each word. "Why can't I just say 'hi'?" I asked. It had been a week.

Abby leaned back, the sofa creaking as she shifted position. "It's not a bad opener; 'Hi, it's Elle.' No kiss though."

"But he put an 'x' on his post-it." I shook the sticky yellow square of paper at her. We'd analysed that too.

"So? You don't know how you feel about him, and you don't want to set expectations. No kisses in the text. Not yet."

"Does it really matter?"

"Fine!" Abby jumped off the sofa and stalked to the kitchen to retrieve a chocolate bar from her stash. She'd selected a Galaxy family-sized bar, so I knew she was annoyed with me. If I didn't agree with her soon, she might start stress baking and then I'd stress about the mess in the kitchen and start trying to clean up after her and then both get stressed. It was part of our pattern. That didn't mean I had to like it.

Instead, I walked to my room and selected one of my many

empty notebooks. I trailed my hand along their spines, searching for the perfect one to suit what I wanted to write in it. My fingers stopped on a notebook bound in scarlet faux leather. I pulled it out and ran the pads of my fingers over the hearts embossed into the front cover. I wasn't sure when or why I had bought it, but it would be perfect.

I returned to the sofa and sank back down into the sagging cushions, holding up the notebook in triumph. "I need to brainstorm."

Abby put down her chocolate bar and leaned forward. "Yes! That's what I'm talking about. Let's get to the heart of this thought cake."

I wagged a finger at her. "This is my notebook, my rules. I'm not doing any thought cakes." My friend's unique approach to answering people's problems in her online agony aunt column had won her a large following, but I wanted something more logical than talking about icing thoughts and gooey centres.

I paused on the first page, pondering what to name this notebook. It was a big decision, to christen a pristine page with a title, knowing I'd only use the notebook for this single topic. Love? Too big. Liam? Too stalkerish. I settled on Dating.

Satisfied with my title, I turned to the second page in my book – I only ever write the title of the contents on page one – and started making a list of all the reasons to avoid a relationship and call it off with Liam before we even started anything.

Abby let me do that until my page was full, then she made me start a new list of all the reasons why it was a good idea to go on a date with him on the next page. When I faltered, she helpfully added her own until it outweighed the list of cons I'd made.

I still counted each point and wrote the total at the top of each page. Abby nodded like that meant we'd made a decision. When I suggested I attribute a weighting to each point, because let's be honest, Liam having good hair was not equal to opening my heart up for potential heartbreak, Abby told me I was overthinking it, broke off a large chunk of chocolate and turned over the page.

With a sigh, I asked her what the new page was for.

"Working out how much therapy you need."

I chuckled at that. I probably did need something in that area, but I'd only cleared my overdraft last month, and the oversized rent on our postage stamp of a shared flat plus my commuting costs took a big chunk of what was left. My hands itched to check on my financial progress spreadsheet and see if I could eke out any savings elsewhere to speed up getting a deposit for a place of my own – in my mind, the youngest director in the Bathory Corporation lived on their own in a modern flat in the city, so as well as my career goal, I was saving to get a mortgage. According to my latest projections, if I didn't eat, I could get there in ten years.

On the plus side, I got free counselling from the company,

which was sort of like therapy, and subsidised organic meals in the canteen. Maybe I could start hustling in London pool halls, too. No. Where would I find the time when I had to focus on my accountancy studies outside of work.

While I was contemplating my future, Abby had found a pink pen topped with a fluffy feather and leaned towards my notebook. I pulled it away, out of her reach. I was funny about new notebooks and didn't like to share and this one felt personal, literally, since it was devoted to my about-to-be-existent love life.

"Do you want me to get you one of my emergency notebooks?" I asked, clutching the red book to my chest.

Abby sighed. "No." She checked her phone. "Let's brainstorm opening texts because you need to send it before nine p.m. unless you want to risk getting into booty call territory."

"What does that mean?"

Abby gave me a pitying look. "If you text a guy late at night, out of the blue, it means you want a hook up."

"But nine o' clock isn't late, you're always telling me I need to get a life."

"It's late for you, and he probably works stupid hours too, so maybe you've found someone who wants to be in bed by nine." She waggled her eyebrows at me and I swatted at her with my book. "Besides, I know you, you'll overthink it and not send it until gone eleven; prime booty call territory."

"Fine." I gave up. "I'll send it before nine."

The opening credits to *Celebrity Love Peninsula* sounded on the TV and Abbey handed me a row of chocolate squares as we settled down to watch the recap.

"I cannot believe he did that," I said, my eyes on the TV.

"Don't even think about distracting me," Abby said. "We are sending that text. You can brainstorm all you want, but you need to send something. Tonight. You've already left the poor guy hanging on for a week."

"Fine." I snatched up the notebook and got scribbling with Abby adding her thoughts over my shoulder while she kept one eye on the drama unfolding on the screen.

When we'd finished, I had a simple line ready to go:

Hi Liam, it's Elle. Here's my number.

Not exactly Shakespeare, but Abby promised me it hit the mark between not being too keen but showing him I was interested.

Liam clearly didn't know any of her rules because I saw the three dots that meant he was replying come up straight away.

Chapter 28

Decisiveness is one of the defining factors of my success. I didn't get to where I was by shilly-shallying about not making decisions.

Elizabeth Bathory – *The First Disrupter*

I showed my screen to Abby. She squealed and made grabby hands that meant I had to make sure she didn't get my phone because she'd type something so not me I wouldn't be able to undo it.

Instead, I picked up Nibbles and headed for my room. Leaving the shaggy hamster to run around my bare floor, I stared at the phone.

"Don't overthink it!" Abby shouted from the living area before the theme tune for *Celebrity Love Peninsula* filled the flat. They didn't have to worry about confusing text messages, but then, their show was built on forced proximity and lots of alcohol and nudity which, while entertaining, wasn't the best foundation for a relationship.

Liam's reply came at that moment with the chirpy beep that announced an incoming text.

Elle! Glad you got my message. What are you up to tonight? x

Tonight? I tapped my hand against my leg and bit my lip. I couldn't go out tonight. I was already in my slouchy t-shirt and I'd promised to watch bad TV with Abby. Was he even asking me out tonight? Or did he genuinely want to know?

Ugh.

I threw my phone onto the covers and cradled my head in my hands. So much uncertainty and we weren't even in a relationship, not even a proto-relationship. I snatched up my phone. I had to say something, but I didn't want to seem like I wasn't keen or that I didn't have a life.

Elle: Hanging out with my flatmate. You?

Liam: Just crashing at home. I'm wiped after work.

Elle: Me too.

Liam: How do you feel about pizza?

Elle: Love it. You?

I winced. Stupid question. He wouldn't have asked me if he

hated the stuff. And now I'd used the word 'love' in a text. Abby would tell me off for that. Probably. This was all too difficult. My thumbs hovered over my screen, ready to say that this had all been a mistake and I couldn't go out with him, and he should ask someone else when he replied.

Liam: Cool.

Cool? He made texting look effortless. I scrambled to think of a reply and ended up with:

Elle: What's your favourite topping?

I was pleased with that; a non-invasive question that kept the conversation going – something Abby had said was important. But those three little dots didn't come up to show he was replying. Was that too banal? Questioning everything, I threw the phone down and sank onto the floor with Nibbles.

He nuzzled my hand, looking for more treats. When I told him I didn't have any, he started trying to shred my t-shirt. I pulled the determined hamster away and stroked his soft fur.

"At least I don't need to guess anything where you're concerned," I told him.

Nibbles looked up at me. I swore the giant hamster could understand every word. There was something knowing in his beady black eyes. And then he bit my finger, to show me who was boss and punish me for not having any treats.

With a sigh, I put him in the part of the cage that went into my room through a combination of twisting plastic tunnels that wound through the hole in the wall that the landlord had promised he'd fix before we moved in. He hadn't, but I'd plugged it with one of Nibbles' tunnels and it meant the hamster had a larger run, so we'd stopped complaining and the landlord had never mentioned it again.

With Nibbles secure and the text messages sent, I rejoined Abby in the lounge area to watch the rest of the TV show, but I didn't really concentrate on Brian or Candice or any of the other contestants and I called it a night as soon as the programme finished.

Liam still hadn't texted back and I knew I wouldn't get to sleep worrying about why he hadn't replied, so I took out my sudoku book to occupy my brain while I tried to relax. It wasn't real maths, but it was logic, which was similar. There was only one answer and as I slotted the digits into the grid, my mind stopped racing and numbers filled my thoughts. Why couldn't life be this simple?

A scuffle told me that Nibbles had escaped from his cage. Sometimes I wondered why I bothered to shut him in; the wily hamster could get out of anything, no matter how cunning the locking mechanism was.

I retrieved him from where he sat on the windowsill, focused on something outside. A loud crash made me jump and I peered out through the blinds into the London night. The humming lights from the local corner shop and the Thai restaurant below us lit up the road and a dark shape disappeared around the corner. I shivered, pushing away my first thought that it was a killer on the prowl for graduates in London apartments. It was probably someone who'd drunk too much trying to get home.

I closed the blinds again and put my escape artist hamster back in his cage then I stared at the stained ceiling for a long time, thoughts about work and Liam chasing each other around my mind for a long time before I fell asleep with my sudoku half finished.

Chapter 29

People with real power don't need to make threats.

Elizabeth Bathory – *The First Disrupter*

As I passed the growing group of protesters outside the front entrance to the Bathory Corporation, huddled together against the springtime shower, I heard footsteps pounding behind me. I span, my hands up. Precious had drilled me twice a week and, while I wasn't strong or great, my muscles had learned what to do when someone approached me from behind.

It took a fraction of a second for me to realise that anyone catching up to me outside the office was probably a colleague or a vampire looking for a quick drink, and I couldn't assault one of them. Another millisecond and I recognised Liam heading in my direction, ignoring the protestors.

I smoothed down my hair. I had no idea what to say in this situation or why my heart flipped in my chest.

Before I could say anything, Liam gave me a lopsided smile. "Sorry about last night, I just sort of fell asleep."

"They must be working you hard in IT."

"You have no idea." His gaze searched my face. "So, are we OK?"

"We're good. We were just texting."

"I promise that you'll have my full attention when we're on our date." His gaze turned intense, and my cheeks heated.

"So, what are we doing on our date?" I aimed for playful banter, but it sounded like an interrogation.

"I thought something classic like dinner."

"I do like dinner."

"It's an important meal," he agreed as we climbed the steps and entered the building.

A roar sounded outside, and we both turned to see what was going on. A sleek black car had pulled up and a chauffeur in a grey suit got out and stood waiting.

The doors to the office swung open and Elizabeth Bathory stepped outside, large dark sunglasses hiding her eyes from the early morning pre-dawn light.

Liam tensed and grabbed my hand, pulling me to one side as the CEO gave the tiniest huff of annoyance before fixing her face into a smile and giving the people gathered outside a small smile.

"Vampire bitch!" someone called.

"Taking our jobs!"

"Go back home!"

Elizabeth Bathory prowled down the stairs, and everyone fell back as if they knew they were in the presence of an apex predator. She paused by one protestor who quaked on the bottom step. "Careful. This is private property. I'd take a step back if I were you before someone calls the police for trespassing." Her tone was clear and friendly, as if she were offering advice.

The man gulped and backed away. "Was that a threat? She threatened me?"

"If I threatened you, you'd know about it." With that, she swept into the waiting car and the chauffeur shut the door behind her before driving off.

I sighed. "She's amazing."

"If you like that sort of thing," Liam said with a shrug.

We walked into the office, the crowd lapsing back into mumbles and grumbles now the vampire had gone.

"What's not to like?" I asked. "She's a strong woman, the original She-EO, heading up the Bathory Corporation for four hundred years and turning it into a global conglomerate. She's everything I wish I could be."

Liam stopped, his shoes squeaking on the tiled floor. "You want to be a vampire?"

I thought for a moment. The answer seemed important to him, and I wanted to be truthful. The pain of being bitten lanced through my thoughts and I brushed my fingers over my neck. Did I want to have to change to get what she had? "No,"

I said, and I meant it. "It's not the vampire part, it's everything else. I wish I could have her confidence, her poise, the respect she commands, the success she has. Everyone wants to be in her orbit. I want that."

"Not everyone wants to be in her orbit," Liam muttered.

"What's your problem? She's your boss, you should be grateful to have a job here. I know I am." My annoyance broke through. This was all I ever wanted, and it hurt that someone I cared about hated it.

He raked his hand through his hair. "I don't want to fight, Elle, but this is a job to me. That's all it is. I'm here because I have to be and if I didn't," he exhaled and looked off into the distance, "if I didn't, I'd be free to choose where to work."

"Why don't you leave then? If you hate it so much?" I started striding off.

"It's not that simple."

I wanted to tell him to stop following me but we were both going to the basements and it felt too petty to ask him to wait for the next lift.

"Sure, it's that simple. You can quit, get another job. That's the free market for you."

He smiled and shook his head. "The free market economy for employment doesn't take into account curses."

I snorted as we got into the lift, sure he was joking. But when I studied his face, he was serious. "Curses? Seriously? Come on."

"You believe in vampires, but you won't believe in curses?"

"Vampires are real, we see them walking around all the time, but what? You're telling me that you're cursed to work here?"

He nodded.

No wonder he hated it here if he was forced to work in the IT department because of some spell. "So, how do you break a curse?" I frowned, my knowledge of supernatural stuff was limited to what I'd learned on the job, and no one had tried to curse me yet, so I knew nothing about them.

"We could try a kiss." Liam leaned forward, his gaze heating.

I squinted up at him. "Like in the films? Don't I have to be your true love for that to work? Or a princess?"

He raked his hand through his short, dark hair before pushing his glasses up his nose. "Do you always overthink things?"

"Oh, it was a joke."

"Worth a shot."

I laughed and almost forgot what we were talking about. "Stop trying to distract me. There has to be a way to break your curse. What are you cursed to do anyway?"

The elevator dinged and he slipped out. "This is my stop."

I held the door. "Come on, you have to tell me."

Liam shook his head. "Another time."

"Really?"

"I've got to find some way to keep you interested." He grinned, took my hand and lifted it to his mouth, his lips grazing my knuckles and sending a searing heat running up my arm. "Until we meet again, Princess Elle."

I shook my head in mock annoyance, squeezing his fingers to show I was joking before allowing the doors to close. Mentally, I added researching curses to my to-do list.

Chapter 30

What you call yourself is important, it tells everyone who you are.

Elizabeth Bathory – *The First Disrupter*

I nodded to the man and woman in overalls affixing a new sign to the wall in the basement. It read; Archives Collective.

It made sense they'd chosen collective when they'd rebranded departments; the Bathory Corporation wanted us all to assimilate with them until there was nothing left outside of work. Just like the Borg in Star Trek. *Thanks, Abby, for being the reason I knew that reference*; like I wasn't a big enough geek without knowing Star Trek.

Ahmed glowered at the workers, his arms folded over his chest as he watched them work.

"You don't like the new name?" I asked, unpacking my laptop bag and hanging up my coat, leaving a small puddle dripping onto the floor thanks to classic British springtime weather.

I checked the display wheel of books out of habit and wasn't disappointed to see a snail fighting a knight in the corner of a text. *Nice one, George.*

"The Archives does not need a noun to follow it," Ahmed said, interrupting my perusal of the medieval picture. "We are not a collective, we protect a collection."

The sign up, the man polished the gleaming plastic while the lady packed away their tools. When they were done, they headed off without a second look in our direction.

Ahmed waited until the lift doors closed before flicking his fingers at the sign. It disappeared, replaced by a brass plaque that read; Archives. He sighed, "Much better."

I grunted in acknowledgement, and he narrowed his eyes at me. "You are not still angry about the Book of the Dead, are you?"

I wasn't annoyed at him. My mood was soured by lack of sleep, and the strange conversation with Liam and I still wasn't sure if we had a date or not; he'd mentioned dinner, but not when or where. But I couldn't let his reference to the Book of the Dead pass. "You told me to open it!"

"And you would agree to follow any order someone gives you if they outrank you? Psh, youngling, you have much to learn. Do you think that Alexander the Great would have conquered Egypt and parts of India if he had not questioned his elders? Yes, he was a spoiled son of a donkey at times, but he questioned everything."

Wait. "You knew Alexander the Great?"

"Alexander the Spoiled would have been more apt. Always taking what did not belong to him and thinking he was so clever when he cut through that knot as if a child could not have thought of that." Ahmed clicked his tongue at the memory before waving his hand. "That is of no importance. The point is that you must be growing up. Take responsibility for your own actions. Do not follow blindly."

"So Alexander the Great wasn't a genius?"

Ahmed snorted, which told me what he thought of that historical figure.

"Who else did you know?" I asked, curiosity overriding my desire to sit on my own and tap at my database.

Ahmed thought for a moment. "Have you heard of Magnus of Carthage?"

I shook my head.

"Good. He was an imbecile. I told him that calling down lightning strikes upon the tower where he lived was a poor idea, but he was convinced it would inspire fear." A slow smile crept over Ahmed's face. "It did, of course. He wet himself before jumping out of the window to escape the flames. And that's how I ended up stuck in a lamp, buried in rubble for a hundred years." Shaking his head, Ahmed pulled at one of his long moustaches. "Anyways, the point is; don't bear grudges. Do you think I am upset about that jelly prank?" His eyes glowed and sparks flew off his ruby waistcoat.

"Er, you don't seem happy."

Ahmed forced a smile. "No, no, it was a good joke. So good, that when I find out who did it, I will be happy to repay the favour. Tit for tit, yes?"

"Tit for tat, I think."

He waved my correction away and turned to the catalogue. "You are finding this of use?"

I nodded. "If I stand over here it turns when I ask for items."

The djinni frowned at me. "It does not work when you are close?"

"No. Maybe it doesn't like me or is worried I might damage it. I read up on how to handle old books and got some protective gloves, but," I shrugged, "I guess it prefers distance."

"Hmmm," Ahmed said, his golden gaze turning bright with curiosity. "And your project is progressing well?"

"Oh yes," I nodded and opened my laptop, "Dedomena gave me some sort of supernatural R Fae ID tags and they're helping with the location. If anyone takes anything from the Archives, an alarm will sound."

Ahmed laughed. "No one can take anything from the Archives, and if they tried, more than an alarm would sound."

"Well, this way, you can search more easily instead of having to go into the maze to check if something's there. You can look it up."

"That is the purpose of the catalogue." He patted my

shoulder.

"But, it would save time." I stopped, not liking the whiny note that crept into my voice. Was my database really a good idea if I had to work so hard to convince him? Still, I had to believe in myself, choose power or something. That was what my counsellor had said, so I forced myself on. "Anyone in the company who needed to know wouldn't have to ask you, they could look it up."

Ahmed gave the bright red phone on the wall a strange look. "If you can stop that infernal thing from interrupting my day, then good luck with the project, Elle." He twirled his moustache and made the little step he did before he disappeared into the inkwell.

"Wait!"

Ahmed turned, his eyebrows raised in a quizzical expression that made me want to laugh.

"Do you know anything about curses?"

His eyes lit up. "Who do you want to be cursing?"

"What? No, no one, nothing like that." Ahmed's shoulders fell. "Just someone said something about curses, and I was wondering if they were real…" I trailed off, not wanting to share more about Liam's predicament.

Ahmed scratched his chin. "Curses are real, but they take strong magic and require real intent. Without knowing more, I cannot be of help."

"What about a curse to keep someone working somewhere they didn't want to?" That couldn't get tied back to Liam, surely.

"Ah, an indenture. That is one type of curse although it is more accurate to say it is a contract. I think we have a book about indentures…" Ahmed clapped his hands, and the catalogue shuddered on its spot on the display wheel. I took a step back and sure enough, its pages started flipping. "Here." He then said something I couldn't pronounce.

I sighed. "I don't speak whatever language that was."

"Schools do not teach ancient Egyptian? What a world. Well, I will see if I can find any other books in a more modern language." The phone rang, cutting into the deep comforting silence of the Archives. Ahmed glared at it. "And you can hurry up to break my indenture to that infernal phone."

He disappeared into his inkwell.

I decided to take that as positive reinforcement and answered the call. "Hello."

"I'm after a thing of great cultural interest."

"Can you be any more specific?"

"It's female, we think."

"Like a statue?"

"With speckles on its cheek."

Oh no.

"And a habit of throwing up when nervous."

"Piss off, Tristan."

He guffawed down the phone.

"Why are you calling?" I demanded.

"Have you seen Precious?"

"Not today."

He huffed and changed the topic. "What's a genie's favourite drink?"

I sighed. It was best to humour him so we could both get on with our days. "What?"

"Djinn and tonic." He burst out laughing.

My lips twitched. That was kind of funny. "Not djinn-ger beer, then"

"Nice one, Speckle." I hated that nickname. "How about abs-djinn-the?"

"Got it all out of your system? That was terrible."

"I'll think of something else. Anyway, guess why this bloke is late with his loan payment."

"Is this a joke?"

"No, it's one of my underwriting cases. He only fell off the bloody balcony. Twice. Broke his leg and couldn't send a cheque in. Bloody hilarious."

"Goodbye, Tristan." Idiot.

I went back to entering objects in the database, attaching the tags that Dedomena had provided and cross referencing with the analogue catalogue. It kept me busy for the rest of the day and when I checked the time, it was gone seven o'clock.

I stretched out, announced that I was calling it a night and packed up. In the lobby, I paused on one of the fabric-covered benches to stretch and tell Abby I was on my way.

A ding announced that the elevator had pulled up and I glanced that way and dropped my phone. Precious had Tristan pushed up against the mirrored interior of the lift. And they were kissing.

201

Chapter 31

Never give away your power.

Elizabeth Bathory – *The First Disrupter*

I gaped at my two work friends embracing in the elevator. On company time. I blinked twice as if that would erase the image from my eyelids. It didn't. Precious glanced my way and shoved away from Tristan. I spun on my heels and walked in the opposite direction.

"Elle, wait!" Precious called.

I ignored her, too embarrassed to think clearly.

The orc caught up with me easily and placed a hand gently on my shoulder. I stopped and turned to face her.

"I'm sorry – I didn't know – I shouldn't have – I won't tell anyone–"

"Hey, it's cool. I wanted to tell you, but it's Tristan." She emphasised his name as if that explained everything. In a way, it did. He was the sort of friend you were slightly embarrassed to have, let alone snog in an elevator.

"So, you and him are… an item?" I couldn't keep the disbelief out of my voice.

"No. Gods no! Me and him." Precious shook her head. "We're messing around. It's hard working here, I need some stress relief."

"And you chose Tristan?" I said his name with the same emphasis she'd used, my brain refusing to make a connection between the two of them.

"As a person, he's a total numpty," she agreed, "but we've got a strict no talking rule. It's physical only."

"But Tristan?"

Precious shrugged. "I know what I want."

"But…Tristan?" I was stuck on repeat.

Her shoulders fell. "I know. I shouldn't want him. He's so pathetic, and not in a cute way. It started out at the end of year do, when I wanted revenge for him stealing our clothes…" I hugged my chest as I relived the embarrassment of walking back to the audit site in my underwear. "But his weakness is so endearing. I want to both protect him and throttle him at the same time. It works."

"Snookums, are you done yet?" Tristan called from where he stood in the lobby adjusting his hideous tie.

Precious whirled round. "I told you not to call me that or I'll throw you on the floor."

"Promises, promises," he leered.

I fought to keep the bile from my throat at their flirting, if that was what you called whatever this exchange was.

"Dzrak off, I'm talking to my friend."

"Whatever," Tristan said. He winked and hefted his laptop bag onto his shoulder. "You know where to find me when you're done." He swaggered out of the building.

Precious watched him go, a smile curving her red lips. She had it bad.

"So, you're not together, like in a relationship?" I asked.

"No."

"Why didn't you tell me?"

"It's Tristan."

We were going round in circles. I decided to change it up. "If you're happy, then I'm happy for you."

Precious sagged. "I'm glad."

Did my opinion really mean that much to her? "I mean I still think he's a total dzrakhead, but if anyone can handle him, you can."

"That means a lot."

"So, do you want to catch him up?"

Precious licked her lips. "Nah, let's make him sweat. He's better when he's needy." She clocked my screwed-up face and explained, "He works harder. Let's get a drink, then I'll go get him."

Chapter 32

It's important to have a mentor, someone who can provide advice and guidance, someone who can support you as you develop your career. A good mentor can be the difference between corporate success or failure.

Elizabeth Bathory – *The First Disrupter*

I rolled my shoulders as I waited for Newton's previous meeting to end. He was a senior executive advisor – whatever that meant – but unlike most executives here, his office was on one of the upper floors rather than in the executive basement, well above the Archives, with lots of dark panelled wood lining the halls and paintings that looked like Renaissance masters hanging from brass picture rails.

I was so busy studying one of the dudes in a black robe with a frilly white shirt wondering why he looked so familiar that I didn't notice the door open.

Kylie stumbled out, her hand at her neck and a wild, vacant

stare on her face.

"Kylie? Are you OK?" I stood, wondering what had happened.

She stiffened her spine in an instant and sneered down at me. "I'm fine. Why wouldn't I be? Didn't you see the rebrand. It's gone perfectly and I'm top of my year. I was just chatting through options with Isaac."

I nodded, reminded that graduates competed against each other for jobs. There were no guarantees on the Bathory Corporation graduate scheme, we were all up against one another. We'd already lost half the graduates at the placement one Reaping event, and there weren't enough jobs on offer at the end of this for all of us. That was how we knew we were the elite, the best of the best. We'd made it through the rigorous recruitment process, and we still had to prove ourselves so only the cream of the graduates made it through to full-time positions.

"Why are you here?" Kylie narrowed her eyes at me. As my buddy, she was meant to share what she'd learned and help me on the scheme, but she'd taken an instant dislike to me. I thought maybe we'd made some progress when she'd said she needed to soften her image, but it looked like we were back to square one. "You're in the Archives, not in his reporting line." She took a step forward. "Are you here to complain about me?"

I huffed out a breath and stood my ground. "Not everything is about you. And who I meet is none of your business."

Kylie bristled at that, pursing her lips and flipping her hair. "I thought you were one of the good ones, but if you think you can beat me to one of the roles this year–"

"He's my mentor." I cut her off. I hadn't even thought of applying for any jobs this year and ending my graduate placements early. I was still studying for my accounting qualification and learning loads and tying myself down to a job now would give me certainty, but it would close down my access to the courses the graduate scheme offered, not to mention the mentorship. Besides, there weren't any risk management jobs on offer and that was where I wanted to be, that was where I knew I could put my mathematical background to use and climb to director level before I was thirty.

Newton appeared in the doorway and looked down his large nose at both of us. "Miss Bruma, in. Miss Smith, why are you still here?"

"Sorry, sir." Kylie bowed her head before flipping her long hair and stalking off.

"Are you making enemies, Miss Bruma?"

I sighed. "Everyone's out for themselves here."

He nodded and walked past me to take a seat behind his imposing desk; a sturdy walnut antique with a red leather top embossed with gilt patterns. It spoke of power and age and reflected its vampire owner.

Above us, a model of the solar system rotated on the ceiling while maps lined one wall and a giant eye stared down from on top of a filing cabinet. A moon lamp also graced his desk, sitting on top of stacks of handwritten papers. That was new since last time I'd been here. Perhaps it was related to his solar studies.

Newton steepled his fingers, regarding me over the top of them for a long time. "I am glad to see you have learned that much. How are your studies faring?"

"Good. I've signed up for three papers this session and I'm on track." It was nearly killing me keeping up with the study as well as working all hours on my database project, but there was no way I'd show weakness to my mentor. The last time I'd done that, he'd told me I could leave. "The exams are in June, right at the end of my placement."

"And your placement is going well?" It sounded like he was reading off some internal checklist.

I nodded. "I'll admit I wasn't sure about the Archives at first, but I'm learning a lot there – more than I would in other departments – and Ahmed has given me leave to start a database. I won't be able to map the entire collection, but I'm making a start. I think it will be a useful pilot and I hope they'll continue the project after I leave."

"Ahmed has let you digitise the Archives." Newton arched one eyebrow. "You must have made quite the impression."

Hah. I wasn't a null after all. I was good at my job. I lifted one shoulder, aiming for a nonchalant shrug. The amused tilt to my mentor's lips told me I hadn't quite succeeded. I tried to channel my inner Elizabeth Bathory. "One does one's best."

Now he was outright smiling at me, his fangs shining in the light of the artificial sun hanging from the ceiling. "I can see this placement has been good for you. Perhaps you'll succeed here after all."

I let out a breath. Maybe this wasn't so bad.

Newton turned to some papers. "Was there anything you needed to discuss?" He sounded bored.

I shook my head then paused. "Actually…"

"Yes?"

"Do you know anything about curses or indentures?" I might as well use all resources at my disposal to help Liam.

"I am a vampire and a man of science, not a witch. Have you been cursed? I'm sure that's against company policy. And you're mine." His eyes narrowed and I glimpsed a flash of the dangerous predator that lurked behind his curled wig. I held myself still. "An assault against you is a strike against me. Who cursed you?" He flashed his fangs, and I shrank back.

"No one. It just came up. In the Archives." I didn't want to lie but seeing this animal side to my composed mentor was unnerving. It reminded me that I was prey in a world of predators and all I could do was build my knowledge and experience until I could show my worth and hold my own in this place.

Newton licked his lips. "Fine. But if anyone harms you, you let me know."

I squirmed in my chair.

"What is it?" He was back to sounding bored.

"One of the managers drank from me in the cafeteria."

He tapped his finger on the desk. "That is permitted. Technically. Did it happen today?"

I shook my head. "It was a while ago. I think they're avoiding me more than the other graduates."

"Really?" Newton raised an eyebrow. "And why would vampires avoid you?"

My cheeks flushed and my gaze stuttered away from him, landing on the model of the sun on the ceiling. "They say I taste awful."

"Fascinating." My eyes darted back to my mentor's face in time for me to see his gaze flick to my neck.

I sighed and tilted my head. One of the perks for vampires, and one of the downsides for graduates, was that we were essentially snack boxes on legs. And no one had drank from me this week.

Amusement flashed over Newton's face. "Very clever. Many vampires relish the reluctance. I theorise that it is a predatory feature, but it is much less diverting if you offer yourself up."

"I can't fight you." I shrugged.

"Who am I to turn down a free meal?" He moved so fast, he was at my side before I knew he'd stood up. He ran a cold finger down my neck before sinking his fangs into my skin. There was a flash of pain before whatever dulling agent was in vampire saliva kicked in and my neck turned hot as he drank. It was over in a moment. "Are you sure you are human? You taste repulsive."

I shouldn't have cared, but my face flushed.

And then he pulled out a test tube from the filing cabinet and pressed it to my neck, capturing some of my blood before he licked the wound, allowing his saliva to heal the puncture marks. Was storing my blood allowed?

"What's that for?" I asked.

"I wish to run some tests. For scientific purposes."

"Don't I need to agree to that? It's my blood."

"Technically, it is my blood as you offered it to me. But if it arouses such strong emotions in you, then I will refrain from running any tests." He paused and his voice softened, "I make no promises, but it may help find out who you are."

There it was. The temptation to belong somewhere, to have a family. I nodded. Let him run his tests.

Newton tucked the vial away in the small fridge that sat behind his desk and pulled out a canary yellow plaster which he handed to me. I flipped my pass to the yellow side that meant a vampire had already fed on me today.

"Is there anything else you want to talk about?" Newton sat back down and eyed me.

I shook my head, sticking the plaster on my neck and standing.

"Then I shall see you at your placement performance review."

Chapter 33

Do not get on the bad side of a djinni, they can hold grudges that last for centuries. I myself know one djinni who disinterred a body to carry out a petty vengeance.

Ahmed the Magnificent – *The Truth About Djinn*

I was deep into my database project and almost through the pilot section of the Archives I'd been given to play with, which was just as well as my placement was coming to an end, and I was due to start my third secondment the week after next.

I still didn't know where I was going; that was a deliberate part of the scheme to keep us on our toes and make sure we didn't slack off at the end. My performance review was due next week, and then I'd be sent to whichever part of the business I'd been assigned to the week after, assuming I got to stay on the scheme. The Bathory Corporation was ruthless and culled its graduates from their workforce at every change in placement to make sure only the elite got through to the end of the scheme. And even then, there weren't any guaranteed jobs available.

But Ahmed seemed happy with my performance, and Dedomena was pleased to get the contents of the Archives into her data lake, and I finally had a date with Liam.

It had taken some time for our schedules to work out. Between my focus on my project and his exhaustion in the evenings, we hadn't made it out for an evening date. But we'd managed a few lunches and walks to the coffee shop in work time, which always made me feel guilty, as if I should be working and at any moment one of the Bathory Corporation employees might jump out at me and say 'Gotcha!' before handing me my p45 and dashing all my dreams.

But tonight, we were going on a proper date. In the evening. I even had a change of clothes and I'd brought some makeup with me at Abby's insistence. She'd spent many an hour teaching me how to do a smoky eye look, but I couldn't get it to work when I did it myself. Whereas Abby looked like a mysterious goddess, I ended up looking like a bruised panda.

Those were problems for later, though. For now, I had a training session with Precious. I scurried to the empty meeting room Precious had block booked for our lunchtime practices. I liked to think I was getting better, but I couldn't land as much as a punch on her. When I did manage to carry out one of the moves she taught me, I'm pretty sure she let me do it so I didn't get too discouraged. She was a good friend.

"Sorry I'm late," I said as I shut the door behind me.

Precious shrugged, but her eyes gleamed.

I gulped. This was going to be a tough session.

I wasn't wrong. The orc didn't even give me a warning before she lunged at me. I squeaked and ducked back.

"I've been teaching you for months and all you do when someone attacks is squeak. Get your head in the game."

"You took me by surprise."

"An attacker won't wait for permission. Again."

Precious drilled me for the best part of an hour before she called it for today. I stretched out my aching muscles and rubbed my knee – a lot of her techniques involved kneeing someone in the groin, but she always twisted so I got her hard thigh.

"Are you still with Tristan?" I asked as I gathered up my phone.

She shrugged. "He's a good distraction."

"Stress relief?"

Her smile was slow and wicked. "Exactly. You have a date tonight."

I nodded. "I hope it goes OK, but maybe it's not worth it. I mean, I'm so busy with work and I've just finished one set of exams, so I've got about a month before I have to start studying again. Maybe I should focus on my career instead of a relationship."

Precious snorted. "It's one date. And you're so uptight, I

could use you as a bo staff. Relax. Have some stress relief. But first," Precious' nostrils twitched, "shower."

I sniffed myself and grimaced. She was right. I stank. We said our goodbyes and I headed for the onsite changing rooms for a shower, passing Fred doing his strange dance in the atrium. Did that vampire ever work?

After a quick shower using the generic shower gel they had at the office, I realised I hadn't brought a towel with me, so I had to shiver under the hand dryer to dry myself, shifting and waving my hand under it like some sort of demented tai chi master each time it switched off. Once I was merely moist instead of soaking wet, I got into my clothes as quick as I could and tied up my wet hair into a tight bun before checking myself in the mirror.

My daytime makeup had run in the heat of the shower, and I dabbed at it, smearing mascara across my face. More scrubbing and I looked presentable if pale. I'd have to fix that before the date, but it would do for now.

I headed back across the atrium and almost bumped into Fred, still dancing. "Can I get past?" I ducked to one side.

He moved to block me, a pained look on his face. "Can't stop."

"I don't know what this is" I said, stepping to the other side, "but I have to go."

"No," he panted, "I can't stop."

I looked around and saw Ahmed sitting on one of the grey, fabric benches. I don't know how I'd missed him in his scarlet brocade waistcoat and billowing silver trousers. He waggled his fingers at me, and grinned.

I walked over. "Are you something to do with this?"

"I have discovered who placed my inkwell in the jelly."

"You didn't…"

His smile broadened until he looked like a cheshire cat. "You wanted to know about curses."

"You cursed him! That's against the employee handbook." It was one of the weirder sentences in the book, right alongside the line that read: 'Vampires may only drink blood from those humans who don't have a yellow badge'. I should know, I'd studied the entire thing in my quest to understand about curses.

Ahmed lifted one shoulder and studied his nails. "Oopsies daisies. Well, maybe it is more of a spell than a curse."

"OK."

"This curse will keep that moron dancing."

That didn't sound too bad, except then I followed Ahmed's words through to their logical conclusion. Fred would keep dancing forever. He already looked strained. At some point even his vampire strength would give way to exhaustion, and he'd still have to keep dancing. No one would get close enough for him to feed – the vampire was annoying enough without the stigma of doing that stupid dance from the Office all the time – so he'd get bloodlust and hungrier and hungrier and all the while have to dance.

"I got the idea from a sheik who asked me to do this to the man who danced with one of his wives. He wore his feet away to stubs." Ahmed leaned forward, his golden eyes glowing as he tracked Fred's dance.

I swallowed. Every so often I forgot I was in the presence of powerful supernaturals who could kill me with a thought, then something like this brought it right back and made me feel small and insignificant.

"Curses work best when they are tied to something the cursee wants to do, or if it is a bloodline curse then that is more powerful." Ahmed tipped his head to one side.

"And how do you stop it?" I asked, mesmerised by Fred's awful dancing. He shimmy-chased a couple of humans across the lobby. They ran. Not surprising.

"True love's kiss is always a good failsafe."

I stared.

"But some people spend a lifetime looking for their love. You could ask the person who cursed them, or one of their descendants to stop it."

I made a note on my phone. This was good information.

"Or you find a counter curse."

"What's a counter curse?"

"You can ask another magic user to stop it, or a null can do it if they are powerful enough." Ahmed shot me a look before turning back to watch Fred.

I wrote all of that down.

Ahmed stood and clapped his hands. "Have a fun time, Fred."

"You're just going to leave him there?"

"He left me in that jelly." Ahmed spat out the word like it left a bad taste in his mouth and disappeared in a spray of golden sparks.

With a sigh, I called Kylie to explain the dancing vampire in the atrium – this was an HR, I mean, People Collective problem if ever I saw one – before I made for the lifts and took the mundane way back to the Archives.

Chapter 34

Mixing magic with modern technology is challenging, but the results can be well worth the effort.

Maximillian Baskerville – *Magical Liaison Office Internal Notes*

Finished for the day, I escaped to the toilets to change into my dress for the evening, replacing a dull, dark suit with jeans and a loose blouse that Abby had instructed me to wear with at least two buttons undone. It managed to look casual and not over the top, and I was glad I'd resisted Abby's urging to go with something more provocative.

I applied some makeup, foregoing any attempts at a smoky eye in case Liam ended up asking if I'd been in a fight. Standing back, I nodded at my reflection. I looked like someone going out for the evening, ready for a meal or bowling or cocktails, wherever the night took us, whatever Liam had planned. He'd said it was pizza, but was it just pizza or pizza and something?

My need for control seized my gut like a vice, and I forced myself to breathe. It was fine. Liam had planned our date, but he knew me, it wasn't going to be terrible. I readjusted my bag seven times in an effort to reassure myself.

My phone buzzed and I read Liam's text:

Ready for our sky-diving lesson? x

Dzrak. I couldn't do this. Another text came through almost straight away.

Just kidding. Meet you out front x

I needed to have a word with Liam about my control issues. But how to casually drop into conversation that I had neurotic tendencies, liked to plan what was going on in my life, oh and I might have borderline undiagnosed obsessive compulsive disorder?

Precious gave me a nod as I walked out of the bathroom into a deserted lobby. Ahmed had got a call from one of the Executives earlier in the afternoon to take the curse off Fred. The vampire was recovering with a blood pack and a lie down in the emergency coffin room and the djinni was sulking in his inkwell.

"Bit straight-laced, but you scrub up good," Precious

declared after giving me a once over.

"Thanks."

"Code word."

"What?"

"Text me a code word and I'll call you. Give you an out if you need it."

"Oh, I'm sure it'll be fine."

Precious lifted one eyebrow.

I searched my mind for a code word. "How about 'Curse'?"

She nodded and walked off, satisfied, leaving me to my date with Liam.

Chapter 35

Dear Abby, I really like this guy, but he doesn't want to introduce me to any of his friends. I think this could go somewhere, and maybe his friends are all assholes, and he's embarrassed for them. What should I do?

OK honey, let's thought cake this mess. You're with a guy, that's the creamy icing. I get it. Icing's great, but you want more. If you didn't you'd be happy with the way things are. And more means being involved in his life. So yes, it's natural to want to meet his nearest and dearest. He's likely had these friends for life and so, the gooey sour cherry centre of this cake is that, if he doesn't want you to meet them he's either embarrassed of you or he doesn't think what you have together is serious enough to bring you into his inner circle. Sorry to break it to you honey, but it doesn't sound like there's a future here.

Yours cakefully, Abby

Abby Wright - *Ask Abby*

I tapped my foot on the tiles, ignoring the vampires who eyed me as they turned up for their night shifts. Where was Liam? I shifted on the dangerous heels that threatened to kill me if I moved at more than a snail's pace. What was I thinking? If we weren't going for pizza at a fancy restaurant then I was seriously overdressed.

I checked my phone again. One minute to go. Would he be late? I hated people being late for things. Waiting outside doors for counsellor's and social services, and whoever else the foster care system thought I had to see, deign to let me in on their time had left me feeling small and unimportant and determined never to keep anyone else waiting.

I forced myself to take even breaths and rubbed my fingers against my thumb, telling myself over and over that it was fine, all would be well.

"Elle, you made it." I whirled round, ready for the reproach in Liam's voice, but there was none. Instead, his smile was bright and open and he seemed happy to see me. "I was worried we'd have to rearrange again."

I clutched my hands together. "Me too." I smiled back and when he leaned in to kiss me on the cheek, I didn't pull away. This was progress.

"You look beautiful," he whispered against my skin, sending a warm sensation pooling through my body.

I let out a nervous giggle and immediately hated myself for it. I wasn't a simpering fool from a romance novel; I was a confident woman on her way up in the world. I was someone who deserved love, or, if not love, then strong like. If I said it enough times, it would be true.

"So do you," I said, like an idiot. But it was true. He wore a dark green shirt that highlighted his brown eyes and he looked smarter and less tired than when I saw him in the harsh electric lighting of the offices.

"So, how's work?" I asked. *Stupid, banal question.* I needed to up my banter.

Liam didn't seem to mind. He shrugged. "Same as always. One of the vampires discovered a way around our firewalls and I had to mine his computer for evidence for a disciplinary." He shuddered. "You don't want to know how much blood porn I had to sift through."

I froze, unsure what to say to that.

"Sorry. I overshared." Liam raked his hand through his hair, sending it flopping over his forehead in a mussed-up look that made him more attractive. "How are you?" The way he asked it, leaning in and meeting my gaze as if he was genuinely interested in me.

The attention made me nervous. "Same, same. I'll be sorry to leave the Archives actually. I mean, I really want to work in risk, but I've enjoyed my placement and I'm leaving it with a database which is pretty cool…" If you were into that sort of thing.

"Yeah, I saw the data lake link added to the servers for your database. That's awesome. I don't think anyone has tried to digitise the Archives before."

I grinned. He got it. "It's a lot of work, though. You have no idea how many papercuts I've got trying to match ID numbers in our catalogue." I waggled my fingers at him.

Liam took my hand, studied it and, gently, carefully, and brought it to his lips. The kiss was nothing more than a brush of his lips against my fingers, but it seared my skin like an electric shock. He released my hand, and I left it hovering in the air for a moment before bringing it back to my side.

"So is there really a dragon under our building?"

I gave him a playful smile. "You know if I told you that, I'd have to kill you."

"I think I believe you," he said, shooting me a sideways glance.

I laughed and something in my chest unfurled as I relaxed. A quick – well, as quick as I could walk in these stupid heels – walk to the tube station and three stops later, Liam led me to a cozy Italian restaurant that he claimed was one of London's best kept secrets.

I tried not to think that he had taken Rani here before. He was here with me, not his ex.

We walked into the restaurant and took a table at the back in low romantic lighting. There was a single candle on our table and the scent of garlic bread wafted through the air, making my mouth water. A low chandelier hung from the ceiling, threatening to hit anyone walking past. But the servers dodged it with practised ease as they went to and fro carrying steaming plates of pasta and trays of drinks.

This was a place of mismatched charm that I had never expected would exist in London, both quaint and cosy, maybe even kitsch, although I wasn't sure what that meant. I loved it. It was the sort of place where no one worried about the past and only thought of the moment as couples gazed into each other's eyes and whispered romantic nothings. It was the sort of place where people came back time and time again for anniversaries and special occasions. This restaurant symbolised the specialness of ordinary relationships and I couldn't believe I was here. It was everything I never thought I could have, wrapped up in a chequered tablecloth with a linen napkin on top.

I sighed with contentment. I could get used to this. I almost felt like I belonged somewhere, with someone.

"You like it?" Liam asked, a hint of nervousness tightening his jaw.

"Of course I do. You remembered my favourite food is Thai," I deadpanned.

His face fell. "Shoot. We can go somewhere else. Sorry. I thought pizza was a safe bet."

"I'm joking." My banter was awful. "I love it." I reached out to take his hand and gave it a squeeze. When I moved to let him go, he squeezed back with the lightest of pressures that kept our fingers entwined.

"Thank goodness. Rani would never come here with me because she said gluten made her bloated."

So he'd never taken Rani here. Good, this could be our

thing. Except he'd mentioned her on our first date, so was he over her?

Liam grimaced. "Sorry, I shouldn't have mentioned her. I'm such a dork." He pushed his glasses up his nose.

And the gesture was so adorable, that my heart skipped a beat. He was nervous, too. I made him nervous. "I've already forgotten her," I said.

"Me, too," he smiled back at me.

Good. This was a good start. If it went well, this would be the story we'd tell our kids about our first date. Oh no. Too serious, Elle. I tapped my forefinger against my glass to ease my spiralling thoughts, because if this was serious then there would be a first argument, and if we lived together, he'd get to see all my crazy, not to mention my need to alphabetise the cleaning products. Maybe I should send an emergency text to Precious. No. *Breathe.* This was a date. That was all. A date with a guy I liked and who, against all the odds, liked me. We'd take it one breadstick at a time.

The server arrived with a bright glassy smile, ran through the specials – smoked salmon and anchovy calzone or roast veal, neither of which appealed to me – and asked what we wanted before bustling away with our drink order. She returned with almost superhuman speed and placed a bottle of chianti on our table along with two glasses.

Liam poured and I sipped the ruby wine, allowing its warmth to seep into my bones. Perfect.

The evening passed in a haze. We ate pizza, we swapped

work stories and worst Christmas experiences, and favourite films – mine was Rain Man, his was Tron – and all the multitude of small things that people share as they work out, tentatively, slowly, if they might have a future together.

We made plans for another date on Friday. Twice in one week. That felt significant, like he thought I was worth spending time with. It made my heart sing and, for a brief moment, I wondered if maybe work wasn't the most important thing in life, if I didn't have to strive to prove my worth when this man sat opposite me already saw someone worthy of love.

We left the restaurant in a bubble of happiness, my arm linked through his as we strolled back to the tube station, taking the long way, enjoying the London lights that twinkled against the dark sky like stars.

Even the scooters that passed at breakneck speeds, zipping through the lighter nighttime traffic – London roads are never truly empty – were part of this magical night. When one almost crashed into me as they ran red lights with no regard for the rules of the road, Liam pulled me tight to his chest. I could feel the heat of him through his shirt and I shuddered against him, looking up at his dark gaze before my eyes flicked to his lips.

This was it. A first kiss. Technically, a second kiss, if you counted that brush of lips in the Uber. What counted as a first kiss anyway? All the possibilities of a new relationship with none of the baggage. Oh no, I was overthinking this. In this moment, I wanted what other people got without effort. I wanted to forget about not fitting in, about not having a family, about worrying that everything I'd worked so hard to get could be taken in an instant if I let the company down.

His hand moved up my back to stroke my cheek. "Are you alright?" His voice was deep and husky and there was something almost hungry in his eyes.

I nodded, too caught up in the moment to speak. I licked my lips.

Liam bent his head to mine.

I closed my eyes. Our breaths mingled in the cooling night air as our lips touched. It was everything I'd ever dreamed a kiss could be, starting soft before turning into something more. Liam's hands moved to my waist, pulling me closer.

"Who is your friend? Introduce me." A voice cut through our moment like a knife.

Liam tensed. He broke away from me but kept a possessive hand tight around my waist. Something shivered through me; no one had wanted me before, not like this, but he did.

I looked from him to the man who had interrupted us. His boss. I'd seen him in the IT department, but we hadn't been introduced.

Liam moved so his body angled between us. "No."

My heart plummeted to my feet and ice gripped my chest. I looked down at my feet in their stupid high heels. He didn't want to introduce me to his boss. I'd thought we were edging towards something great. I was ready to open up my heart and try for something more. I'd never felt like this before, never allowed myself to feel like this before, but he was ashamed of me. I'd misread him. And I wasn't going to put up with feeling like I wasn't good enough.

I needed to reclaim part of myself or I was going to get into the sort of one-sided relationship I'd promised myself I'd never be in, the sort where one person gave and gave and the other only took. I'd seen it happen a thousand times, in the foster families I'd grown up in, in the other foster kids who latched onto the first bit of affection that came their way. That wasn't for me.

I'd avoided anything like love for so long for exactly this reason, and the first time I'd thought it could be different, I'd found out it was exactly the same. So, I'd leave first.

"Thanks for a lovely evening, but I'd better get going."

Liam whirled round, putting his back to his boss. "So soon." He looked hurt. How dare he look hurt. Behind him, his boss leered, his eyes gleaming in the street lights. Liam sagged.

I nodded and stood straighter. "I'm not sure this is going to work. I've got a new placement coming up and I need to focus on my work. Good night."

With that, I turned and strode to the nearest tube station. I managed to get on the train before I broke down into heaving sobs as my heart shattered into tiny pieces.

My phone buzzed, pulling me from my misery. Was it Abby or Precious checking up on me? I frowned as I stared down at the message – an alert from the Archives. Someone had moved one of the items I'd tagged with the supernatural R Fae ID labels out of its place. Maybe it was just George or Ahmed.

The need to check tugged at my gut. I'd head into work, check and go home and break into Abby's emergency chocolate stash.

Chapter 36

Djinn are tied to their containers until freed. A common misconception is that whoever holds their vessel controls them, but the truth is worse, in a way. While the person in possession of the container might not control the djinni inside, they can prevent them from ever leaving.

Ahmed the Magnificent – *The Truth About Djinn*

s I entered the Archives, the hinged section of the desk was balanced upright and I heard voices from the stacks. I squinted into the dark corridors. "George?" I asked as I walked through the desk.

No answer. Of course, they were at a wrestling match this evening. But why was the display wheel pushed to one side?

"Ahmed?" I looked over at the inkwell. Which wasn't there.

The hairs on my arms stood up. Something was wrong. Ahmed's inkwell was always in place. I pulled open drawers in the desk in a frantic search. Maybe some vampire had put him in jelly again as a prank.

When I couldn't find him, I sank against the desk, trying to control my breathing. I tapped my fingers to my thumb in a familiar repetitive rhythm as my mind raced.

There was someone in the Archives who shouldn't be there. They'd done something with Ahmed and there was no sign of George. And they'd messed with my database system.

Important questions spiralled in my head. Questions like; how did they get past the wards? Why hadn't they set off the alarms? And who were they? And, most importantly, what should I do?

There weren't any protocols for this in anything I'd read because Ahmed hadn't thought this situation would ever occur.

My slow brain circled around the word 'security'. Of course, I should ring reception.

With shaking hands, I picked up the antique phone on the wall and started to dial, cursing how long it took to move the circular dial for each number. Why did reception have so many nines in their number?

It wasn't until I was halfway through inputting the number that I realised there was no dial tone. I grasped at the phone line and pulled. It came away to reveal frayed wires.

They had cut the line.

I swallowed. Could I make it back to the lift without them noticing? Then I could get security in person. It didn't feel right leaving intruders in the Archives.

Fumbling in my bag for my phone, I willed it to have signal. Of course it didn't. I typed a text anyway. Precious would know what to do if she got it. I took out my laptop, wincing at every small noise. I'd send an email then sneak out to get security.

I sank to the floor, making myself as small as possible, and opened my computer. Typing as fast and silently as I could, I drafted an email saying I needed help and there was someone in the Archives. It wasn't my most articulate email, but it got the message across.

On a whim, I copied in Precious and Tristan. At least if I got killed down here, they'd know why I didn't turn up to lunch.

Sweat pricked my palms. I couldn't stay here. They — whoever they were — would come back eventually. And if they were powerful enough to break through Ahmed's wards, I had no chance against them. I'd have to risk the lifts and get help from security even if it meant leaving the Archives without a protector.

Who was I kidding? I couldn't protect the Archives. I edged along the wall and crept through the desk, moving as slow as my racing heart would allow while also stepping as fast as I could. Two crouching paces later, I felt my bag snag on something. I turned and my mouth opened in horror as the momentum pulled down the open desk hatch.

"No," I whispered, reaching out to stop the wood crashing into the desk.

I didn't make it in time.

The crack of the wooden hatch banging into its place reverberated around the reception area. I froze for a nanosecond then sprinted for the lifts. The thieves, whoever they were, would hear that. I had to make it to the lift. It was the only escape route.

Never had such few steps felt like so far. The run to the lifts lasted forever as time both slowed to treacle and raced past me.

Behind me, I heard someone hiss something and then brisk footsteps.

I stabbed at the call button with my index finger. "Come on, come on."

I risked a look over my shoulder and gulped. A tall figure swathed in dark clothing now stood behind the desk.

Their eyes widened when they saw me. They hadn't expected anyone.

I jabbed the button again.

By some miracle, the doors opened. I slipped inside as soon as the gap was wide enough for me to squeeze through and rammed my fingers against the door close button over and over as I faced the figure.

The surprise of seeing me had bought some time, but they had come to their senses and climbed over the desk with an elegant fluidity that reminded me of a dancer.

The lift doors began to close.

I breathed a sigh of relief but continued to press the button as if I could somehow sync my willpower with the elevator.

The intruder's eyes narrowed in determination as they closed the distance between the desk and the lift.

The doors continued to close. Five inches to go. Three. Two. *I was going to make it.*

A pale hand shot between the small gap left.

No. I backed away, abandoning the buttons and clutching my laptop bag like a shield.

The lift doors pressed into the slim hand. For a brief moment, I thought the metal doors might crush it. But, of course, there was a safety feature built in and the doors slid open.

The slim female figure stepped forward, blocking the doors from closing again and looked me up and down. "What have we here?"

Their accent was familiar, like the fae I had worked with on my first placement. I swallowed. That placement had ended with their leader trying to kill me when I uncovered their fraud. My entire body shook.

"I work here. I just wanted to check something. But I'm going now. I didn't see anything." I aimed for innocent worker in the hope that she'd let me go.

Instead, she pulled down the half mask that covered the lower part of her face and gave me a slow grin full of pointed teeth. "Oh no, if you work here, then I think you're just who we need."

Chapter 37

Fae are dangerous creatures and should not be underestimated for they are cunning and swift to learn.

Ozark Bumblington – *A History of Fae*

The fae woman hustled me out of the lift and back to the Archives. When my laptop bag caught on the desk – again – she ripped it from my shoulder and flung it so hard, it landed back inside the lift. The doors closed on it, and I swallowed. That bag had all my devices in it. I was totally alone.

My gaze fell on the desk as we passed, searching for Ahmed's inkwell.

"If you're looking for your djinni, he's with us now." The fae smirked down at me and pointed to the nearest stack where a plate of green jelly surrounded Ahmed's inkwell.

For a second, I had the urge to punch her right in her smug face. Then I remembered that I wasn't a tough orc like

Precious, who would no doubt have already hit the fae and would never have let herself get captured in the first place. No, I was small, helpless Elle. I would wait and see what they wanted, try to get as much information from them as I could while I used my brain to seek a solution.

"I found this one," the fae said, shoving me in front of her.

I stumbled.

A taller fae with a foxy face sneered down at me. The pointed nose and dark eyes looked familiar, but I couldn't place him. Maybe he'd worked at Skathi's house when I was auditing it.

"You work in this storage facility?" he asked.

I bristled. This wasn't just a storage facility. I'd had reservations when I'd first started here, but I had learned so much under George and Ahmed's tutelage and I had pride in my work. "I work in the Archives, yes." I pronounced the capital letter with pride.

He smiled down at me, making me feel like prey caught in a trap. "Then you will help us. Where is the Crown of Winter stored?"

I swallowed. They were after the crown. I could lie to them, lead them around the labyrinth until George showed up. It might take hours, but I could lose them in this place. I met his gaze.

"Think very carefully before you speak, little human." The fae in charge pulled out a wavy blade that shimmered in the low lighting. His companions snickered like children in on a prank.

I swallowed and dread prickled along my spine. I nodded. "I'll take you to it."

"Good. Then we can be friends. And, in exchange for this bargain, you may keep your life. For now. Lead on." He waved me in front of him. "Oh, and in case you think you can escape, we'll take your friend with us." He picked up the plate of jelly surrounding Ahmed's inkwell, whispered some words and it floated alongside him like a personal ghost carrying a strange snack.

I faced forward. Having three fae walk behind me, one of them still with the dagger in his long fingers, ranked among one of the most terrifying experiences of my life. I tried to walk normally, but my legs forgot how to take steps and I stumbled more than once.

The first time, the fae laughed and mocked me. By the fifth time, they got annoyed. "Are you sure we should trust her? She can't even walk," asked the female.

"Maybe we should kill her now?" suggested the third. That was the first time I heard his raspy voice. He sounded closer than I thought. Was that his hot breath I could feel on the back of my neck?

"She's human." The one with the knife – their leader – spoke, cutting over the third one's low chuckle. "They value their stupid little lives. We keep her alive." A short pause. "Besides, we can always kill her later."

Great. I stumbled again, too preoccupied with imagining the

myriad ways they might end my life to worry about keeping my balance.

I heard the third one sigh and risked glancing over my shoulder. He grinned at me and drew his finger over his throat. A gasp escaped my lips and I looked away, catching a glimpse of the female counting and noting something down in a book that looked like it was made of leaves.

I turned back to the front. They were planning to count the turns to get out of the labyrinth. I almost laughed. That was their plan for getting out. They didn't know that it changed. My spine straightened. I knew more about this place than they did. I might be small and physically weaker than them, but I had more power here than they thought. A slow smile tugged at my lips as a plan began to form.

Chapter 38

Some fae have a pre-disposition for cruelty and hang on to the antiquated notion that humans are little more than pets or playthings.

Ozark Bumblington – *A History of Fae*

I started moving, leading the intruders deeper into the labyrinth, navigating the twists and turns with an ease that George would have been pleased with.

Behind my back, the fae I now thought of as Killer mumbled something about going round in circles.

I found the confidence to say, "That's how labyrinths work, genius."

The other two chuckled. Killer growled. "Just you wait, little one. I'm going to have a lot of fun with you."

"Back off, Yuni. We need her alive. Besides, if she's got fire like that, maybe I'll keep her as a pet."

A shiver ran down my spine. I'd bet anything that fae didn't treat their pets well. My thoughts tumbled to Nibbles, my pet hamster waiting at home. That giant ball of fluff had stayed with me through thick and thin, through moving families and university. He was always there for me, and my heart ached at the thought that I might not see his chubby face again. I vowed that if I got out of this alive, I'd buy him the biggest hamster treat he could fit in his adorable cheek pouches.

I decided to keep my mouth shut, but when we got to the edge of the restricted section, the leader gripped my shoulder.

"What?" I asked. "We're close."

"You're leading us into an alarm. Nice try. Stay put." He patted my shoulder and shoved me into the shelf while he investigated the glowing red crystals embedded into the wooden racks. A box rattled and I saved it from falling by instinct, clutching it to me.

The fae ignored me as they studied the crystals, muttering about protective spells and discussing the best way to break the wards that protected the restricted section.

I took advantage of the distraction to search the shelves for something that might help me. I hadn't got this far in my database project, and had no idea what we stored just outside the restricted section. Books lined some of the shelves; a copy of Shakespeare's first folio, something by Homer. Nothing I could use, unless I wanted to throw priceless works of literature at the fae.

I considered it for a moment – the tomes were thick and heavy enough to give someone a concussion if my aim was good – but, as I was useless at throwing, all I'd do was damage the books and maybe myself.

A weapon. That was what I needed. I gripped the lead box tighter. Further along the corridor, an orange flame caught my eye. The sword Dyrnwen. If I could get to it, maybe it would lend its fire to my aid. If it thought I was worthy.

First problem first; I had to get to it.

A pleased grunt told me the fae had finished disabling the alarms. Yuni shot me a wicked grin. Hot fear raced up my arms. One step closer to killing me.

"You. Go first," the leader said, hauling me to my feet so fast that I stumbled to get my balance. He shoved me forward.

I fell onto the large paving stones that lined the floor and pushed myself to my feet. The floor was alarmed too. How had I forgotten? Maybe something to do with the serpentine dagger in his hand.

With new determination, I stepped onto the next slab. George hadn't told me what the pattern was so I had to try all the stones. Trying to make it look natural, I walked with a weaving gait, stepping on every stone I could.

"What are you doing?" The female had noticed.

I forced my voice to sound confident. "Looking for the crown. It's somewhere here."

The fae twisted round, paying more attention to the shelves and their cruel eyes gleamed with excitement.

I tried another stone. No alarm. What if they were designed for George's weight rather than lighter people? Surely whoever designed the traps wouldn't have been that stupid…but maybe they hadn't thought that anyone other than a minotaur could navigate the labyrinth.

The fae now had their backs to me as they grew confident and strolled ahead. Keeping my eyes on them, I risked jumping on the paving stone.

Still nothing. But I'd made too much noise. The leader strode over to me. "You're doing something. Why?"

I stared at the floor, unable to meet his gaze.

When I glanced up, he gave me a considered look. "I deduce from your stamping that there are pressure traps under the floor."

The other two fae froze and stared down at the grey slabs under their feet.

"Mel – find out where they are."

The female fae reached her hand into a concealed pocket in her dark outfit and pulled out some baby blue powder. She whispered some words over it and threw it into the corridor. As it drifted to the floor, it lit up certain stones in a wispy scarlet light.

My heart sank. I hadn't got far enough into the corridor to trigger the pressure alarms and now I'd lost that advantage.

"Thank you for your help," the leader said with a sardonic grin.

My stomach tightened at my failure, but I had other tricks to try.

Chapter 39

Never get on the wrong side of a fae.

Ozark Bumblington – *A History of Fae*

I started moving, but the fae leader gripped my shoulder tight. "We wouldn't want you to run off and accidentally set off a trap, would we?"

To my right, Dyrnwen glinted, a flame-coloured light rippling down its blade.

I let my shoulders slump like I had given up and moved with the fae as he took a step forward. Remembering Precious' lesson, I dropped my weight, sinking to a crouch that brought him off balance. I twisted. It didn't shake his grip, but it loosened it enough so I could reach for the sword.

I stretched up on my tiptoes, cursing my small height, wishing I had Precious' six-foot frame. My fingers brushed the sword's hilt. Fiery heat burned my skin with righteous warmth.

"Nice try. But playing with magical swords can get you burned." The leader yanked me away, sending me staggering into the opposite shelves.

My head cracked against the hard wooden stacks and white stars flicked across my vision. Boxes rained down on me. Tears swam in my eyes. I had failed.

The fae pulled me to my feet and twisted my arm behind my back, sending shooting pain along my shoulder. "Do you know where the Crown of Winter is?"

I nodded.

"Show me now. No more tricks. Or I shall let Yuni here have you all to himself."

Yuni turned from where he crouched examining a lower shelf. He gave me a slow smile that told me he was counting all the ways he would hurt me before he finished me off.

My mouth went dry. I didn't have a choice. I had to help them get the crown. Maybe, once they had it, I could do…something. But for now, I had no options.

My fuzzy brain calculated odds of success. Even if I had a weapon, I didn't know how to use it. I was a liability. I couldn't even hold Precious' dagger without breaking the tiled floor. My best chance was to help them. I didn't know if that was logic or the survival instincts of prey in the presence of a predator, like a mouse nodding along with whatever a lion said as it hoped not to get eaten.

"It's along here." My voice came out as a hoarse croak, and I didn't have to fake a wavering step this time. I couldn't walk straight.

Not that it mattered. The fae kept me upright and so tight to his chest that I could feel his raspy breath in my hair.

The other two flanked us, their gazes raking the racks as they sought the crown.

I considered trying to fob them off with another artefact, but I hadn't done enough research on the restricted section to know what would help. My database was focused on the less dangerous sections of the labyrinth.

If only the Archives could help me. The way George spoke about them, there was a sort of connection between them and the labyrinth. Maybe it would extend to all employees. I sent silent thoughts out to the Archives, pleading for help.

Nothing changed. There was no rumble of thunder, no changing of routes. The corridor stayed as it was. Maybe the connection thing only worked for minotaurs.

Fine. I didn't believe in miracles anyway. I believed in working for what you wanted and using your brain to solve problems. So I would get them to the stupid crown and then think my way out of this and come up with something so impressive that Ahmed would give me a glowing performance review.

Not much of a plan. Maybe I'd hit my head too hard.

My gaze locked onto the innocuous box that contained the Crown of Winter.

Chapter 40

The Crown of Winter is one of the royal signatures of the Fae Winter Court. Whoever wears it has a claim to the Winter Throne.

Ozark Bumblington – *A History of Fae*

"**I** take it from your stiffening that we are close." The leader made a gesture and the other two fanned out, searching the shelves. "Look for something that might hide its magical signature. I can't feel anything."

"Cardboard dampens most magics," I said in a small voice.

My reward for contributing was a sneer from the female.

"Here!" Yuni snatched up the ebony box, tilting it this way and that so the gleaming unicorn ivory inlay caught the light, forming twinkling rainbows as he moved it.

These fae weren't as cautious as Ahmed. Yuni opened the box without a second thought and took a fireball to the face.

He fell to the ground, dropping the box as he twisted and pressed his hands to his eyes.

I stepped back from the searing heat, turning my face away as his skin bubbled and the scent of charred flesh filled the confined space.

The box landed on the stones with a heavy thud.

The female – Mel – looked to the leader. He must have nodded.

She toed the case before sprinkling some more of her magic powder on it. I expected a glow of magic, but the powder stayed the same shade of green as it had been when it left her hand.

Mel snatched up the crown's case and, opened it, leaning back in case a second fireball brewed within the small innocent-looking box.

My captor loosened his grip on me, leaning forward, anxious to see what happened. He licked his lips with a wet slapping noise that made me pull away.

No fireball or curse exploded out of the box. The female fae reached in and, with a smile of hideous triumph twisting her perfect features, picked up the Crown of Winter. A cloud of tiny darts exploded into her hands and wrists.

She reared back, screaming. The crown fell from the box and skittered across the floor, disappearing under one of the shelves.

Painful red boils erupted on her skin, and she scratched at them with her pointed fingernails for all of a second before she fell to the floor next to her groaning burned comrade. Her body twitched before thrashing back and forth, racked with convulsions.

A pang of unwanted sympathy twinged my heart. I didn't

want to feel sorry for the thieves, but the poison darts looked like a nasty way to go. I pressed further against the stacks.

The leader abandoned me and lay on his stomach, peering under the shelves for the crown.

And maybe there was something to George's theory that labyrinth magic helped employees, because a box caught my eye.

After a quick glance at the fae to reassure myself he was still occupied, I reached for the small cardboard box. I leaned back as I opened it, just in case it was dangerous, but all that sat inside was one of the polished thunderstones. Great. What use was one of them without its partner?

The box I'd caught when it had fallen from the shelf earlier in the labyrinth pulsed. Holy crap. I flipped the lid off to find the second stone. Thank you, labyrinth.

What had Ahmed said? *Don't put them together.* I had nothing to lose.

Holding my breath, I slammed the two smooth stones together. Nothing happened. Perhaps it had been one of Ahmed's jokes.

That was it. My last hope gone. I had failed. What was the point? The fae had won. It was only a matter of time before he got that stupid crown. I dropped the stones to the floor. I didn't need worthless rocks. The thunderstones clacked together as they fell. Lightning flew from them as a deafening roar of thunder reverberated through the corridor.

I took my chance and ran.

Chapter 41

Dragons are fiercely loyal to those who they perceive to be under their protection.

Aloora Dragonquest – *Talking with dragons, a comprehensive study of cases and contextualism in Draconic*

Behind me, I heard the fae scrabbling on the floor and the moans of pain from Yuni as he squirmed in agony.

I sprinted, giving up on trying to trigger any alarms. I had another idea in mind.

The leader swore. I didn't know if he'd realised I'd got away or if he couldn't reach the crown. Maybe it had skidded all the way to the adjacent corridor. If that had happened, he'd never find it.

A tiny blossom of hope unfurled in my heart.

Then I heard the footsteps. The fae sprinted after me, gaining ground.

"If there is any connection between us, I could really use some help about now, labyrinth," I muttered as I increased my speed, putting everything I had into escaping.

So much that I almost missed the turning. I skidded past, my feet slipping on the stone. I grabbed the corner of the shelves to help me round the bend.

Almost there.

"Xam!" I shouted as soon as I saw her ruby scales. "Break in. Archives. Fae." I panted out the words between breaths, unable to form full sentences.

I didn't hear an alarm. The huge dragon spoke into my mind and raised her head to regard me with curious quicksilver eyes.

"Broken. Wards down." I sucked in gulps of air, still running towards her.

"So this is where you've got to." The fae leader didn't even sound out of breath.

Intruder? Xam asked, whipping her head round to face the fae.

I nodded, pressing into the shelves.

The fae froze as he saw the dragon. He held up his hands and backed away. "I'll just—"

Whatever he'd been about to say disappeared as Xam engulfed him in a concentrated breath of fire. Sulphuric fumes filled the air.

The fae screamed as dragon fire surrounded him. The acrid

scent of burning hair hit the back of my throat making me retch.

"The artefacts," I croaked out. What had I done? In running to Xam to save the Crown of Winter, I had destroyed part of the Archives with flames.

Xam cut off her fire, shutting her ruby red maw with a snap. *Foolish child. You think I would destroy my hoard? Look, all is well.*

I blinked to clear my vision in the smoky air and through hot tears I saw the Archives were untouched. "Magic," I whispered. It never ceased to amaze me how magic defied all the laws of nature and order I had learned. I sank against the closest set of shelves and closed my eyes. All science was magic before you understood it. That yearning to return to the ordered world of academia and find patterns in the chaos pulled at me again.

A sudden laugh burst from my dry throat. I wouldn't have to deal with fae or fire-breathing dragons in university. My laughter turned to sobs and I collapsed onto the stone floor.

A warm, claw stroked my back. *Where are the others, child?*

The others… "Ahmed!" One of the fae held his inkwell. I forced myself to stand and move towards the charred corpse of the fae leader. I approached in a half run, half lopsided walk and bent down next to him.

His flesh had blackened and cracked and through the ash that covered him, I could see pink, raw flesh. He wheezed out a rattling breath. Dzrak. He was still alive. My hands hovered above him, unsure how to help. I had no water and no medical training. The fae managed to open one eye. A single tear coated his eyeball.

He had kidnapped me, joked about killing me and tried to steal from the Archives. I should hate him. But, seeing him like this, my heart panged in sympathy.

A glimmer of something shiny caught my eye. I reached for it, brushing ash motes from the surface. Ahmed's inkwell. The green jelly surrounding it had dissolved into a sticky puddle on the floor from the heat.

I pulled out the stopper, letting out a cry of pain as the hot glass burned my fingers.

"Who disturbs my slumber?" Ahmed appeared in a cloud of blue gold smoke, his eyebrows drawn together in annoyance. "Elle?"

I blinked up at him. "Can you save him?"

His mouth dropped as he took in the burned fae and his nostrils flared at the sulphur stench of dragon fire. "What happened here?"

Chapter 42

Iron does affect fae. For some, it cuts off their connection with magic. For others, it makes them woozy.

Ozark Bumblington – *A History of Fae*

As I explained through choking breaths what had happened, Ahmed placed the fae into some sort of stasis and called in George, who had taken the day off to watch a wrestling match.

Xam added the explanation for using her fire, and Ahmed sighed. "More paperwork. Did they get the crown?"

I shook my head.

"Show me the rest," Ahmed ordered. The usual twinkle in his golden eyes had gone, replaced by all the hardness of a gold bar.

I led the way back to the section I had fled only minutes before. Had it been minutes? So much had happened it altered my perception of time. The theory of relativity in action.

Another problem to mull over when I couldn't sleep, but Einstein already solved that one.

Ahmed zoomed over to investigate the other two fae. The female's lips had turned blue and pulled back from her teeth in a rictus grin. I looked away.

Yuni still moaned, his hands over his eyes. Ahmed put him in stasis too and conjured up a bandage for his burned face.

"Where is the crown?" Ahmed's voice was hard as stone.

I bent down and reached under the stack where it had slid. My fingers closed on thorny wood. A flash of cold ran through my arm before disappearing. Too late, I remembered that only fae from the Winter Court could touch it. I pulled it out as fast as I could and dropped it on the stone.

Ahmed stared at me, his golden eyes narrowed. "It didn't affect you." It wasn't a question.

I gaped down at my uninjured hands. "It was cold to start with, then I dropped it…"

"The Crown of Winter reacts to anyone not of its court." He cocked his head to one side. "Are you a fae?"

"No, I…" I trailed off. Maybe I was a fae. I didn't know my parents, so anything was possible, but surely, I'd have some powers. Fae had magic, didn't they? Hope fluttered in my breast. Maybe I could find my family in the Winter Court. No. I didn't have pointed ears, not like the fae had anyway. I sighed and squashed the old longing down. I'd been down this route before, searching for relatives who didn't exist. But it was too late. Once ignited, the spark of hope is hard to dim.

"I don't know. My parents died when I was young. I was…I don't know."

Ahmed's eyes softened. "Do you feel any magic in you?"

I shook my head, clenching my hands into fists at my side. I had longed for magic so much growing up, telling myself I was a lost fairy princess, or part elf. But there had been nothing. No answering call of power to ease the pain of being alone, no magic that could help me fit in, no magic that could make a new family love me. Nothing.

"Take this." He handed me a cold lump of metal that he pulled from a nearby shelf.

"What is it? Will it tell if I have powers?" I stared at the grey metal, gripping it hard as I willed it to awaken any magic I had in me.

"It's iron. Fae can't touch it without getting woozy in the head." He studied me. "How do you feel?"

"Normal."

"Not fae then."

My shoulders sagged as I deflated.

"Or at least, not normal fae."

"What does that mean?"

Ahmed clamped his lips together as loud footsteps thrummed though the labyrinth.

George ran into the corridor and skidded to a halt. They pulled me into a tight hug. "You're alright."

I wrapped my arms around their solid body, and the tears I'd been holding back started to fall. It was all too much. Liam had made it clear he didn't want anyone to know about us. Fae had broken into the Archives. And I was done.

George looked around, taking in the fae on the floor, my dishevelled appearance and the Crown of Winter still not in its box. With a huff that ran through their entire body, they said, "I'll start on the paperwork."

We returned to the reception area in silence. Ahmed focused on repairing wards as we went and keeping the two fae in their healing stasis. George kept one of their large arms around their body until we made it to the large desk. I sank onto a chair and stared at the wall, numb and spent.

As George pulled out a stack of forms from the desk, Ahmed turned to me. "Take next week off to recuperate." He held up a hand to stop my protests. "Come in on Friday for your end of placement review."

Chapter 43

Performance reviews are an important way to assess if employees are meeting our standards. It gives them the opportunity to grow and course correct, and it gives us a chance to weed out the weak.

Elizabeth Bathory - *The First Disrupter*

I smoothed down my suit skirt as I waited for Ahmed to appear. It was Friday and, as Ahmed had put it, it was time to get my performance assessment 'over and done with'.

I'd spent the week at home, curled up on the sofa watching bad TV with Nibbles for company. Abby had tried everything in her arsenal to pull me out of my slump; ice cream, action movies – I couldn't face a romance – and music, both upbeat and mournful. She'd even offered me sleeping pills, which I'd declined. Then she'd given me space, and I wasn't sure if that was worse than her telling me that Liam wasn't worth it.

Because, yeah, I'd been attacked by the fae, but my body had recovered and the nightmares had dimmed. Now it was just my heartache that was the problem.

Don't get close to people, Elle. Why had I broken my own mantra. I needed to buckle down and focus on my career. And that meant passing this performance review.

Nervous dragons danced in my stomach. I'd saved the Crown of Winter and the reputation of the Archives, but I'd probably broken several company policies to do so. And I hadn't finished my database pilot.

The elevator doors dinged and slid open to reveal Newton. Now it made sense why we were doing this so early in the morning; vampires didn't like the sunlight and the weather forecast promised a bright summer's day later. He caught sight of me, gave a huff of greeting and strode forward. "Where's the djinni?"

I shrugged, stilling my tapping foot.

The vampire scowled.

A golden mist glittered near Ahmed's inkwell and spread until it covered half of the Archives' reception area before morphing into the djinni. His waistcoat today was emerald green covered with a golden pattern of constellations. "Welcome, Elle, to your performance assessment." He followed this with a yawn that rolled around the room like thunder.

Not intimidating at all.

Loud footsteps crashed through the labyrinth. I stood and

tensed, my body moving into a fighting stance as I readied to attack the intruders.

George skidded into view. "I'm not late, am I?" They caught sight of me and scooped me into a hug.

Ahmed coughed. "You are too late to miss my entrance. How do I keep control of this department if you do not have the respect for me?"

George put me down and I gulped in a breath after the minotaur's tight hug. They stepped over to stand at Ahmed's side, caught my eye and grinned. OK, George was on my side.

"It's been a long week, Ahmed, with a lot of paperwork. Perhaps we can commence proceedings?" Newton suggested, cutting through Ahmed's whining.

"Fine." Ahmed fluttered his hand in annoyance. "We might as well get on with it." His waving became more focused and three comfortable seats appeared for my reviewers. They shouldn't have fit behind the desk, but the djinni had done something to the space, or reality, or something and the chairs sat in a neat row facing me. Ahmed's was significantly larger and more thronelike than the others.

George shot me a wink and sat down, making their chair creak. Newton sighed and sank into his chair with a bored expression as if he saw these sorts of theatrics every day.

Ahmed took his time to sit, flapping the long tails of his waistcoat behind him.

I clutched my notebook in my lap and waited.

"So, Noelle Bruma, you are here for your performance

placement review."

"She knows that," George said, rolling their large eyes.

"Yes, but there is such a thing as doing it properly, George." Ahmed let out a breath laced with frustration and his accent thickened. "Look, I do not get the opportunity to do this every day, can you let me be having my moment?" He inhaled and then beamed at me. "In your time here, you have shown fortitude, determination and persistence."

"I believe those are all the same thing," Newton pointed out.

I gulped. Please don't let my mentor wind my boss up so much that it affects my grade. I'd always been a straight A student – apart from that one art class in secondary school – and I didn't think I could stomach a bad review.

My heart jumped in my chest and my fingers itched. I gripped my notebook, so I didn't start my calming exercises. It was too obvious here and I was a successful graduate who could handle anything, not someone who crumpled in a performance review. I raised my chin and tried to convey to Ahmed that I wasn't responsible for anything Newton said, as if I could have any control over a centuries old vampire polymath.

"Fine," Ahmed huffed. "I did have a speech planned, but as some keep interrupting," he glared at Newton who gave a small satisfied smile, "I will say you have passed this placement, Elle, with flapping colours. Congratulations, I am recommending you move on in the graduate scheme."

George clapped. Ahmed glared at them and George sat on

their hands. I gave them a grateful smile. Someone was rooting for me.

"Anything else?" Newton tilted his head towards Ahmed and waited.

The djinni shook his head, his drooping moustache quivering with the motion.

"Then it falls to me to assign your next placement. You expressed a preference for risk management in your response to our survey."

I nodded, holding my breath and leaning forward in my chair.

"Another graduate also named that as their first choice."

My hands balled into fists. So, I wouldn't get to go to risk management. OK, that was fine.

Breathe.

That didn't mean I couldn't get a permanent job there at the end of the scheme, I'd just have to adjust my plans.

Breathe.

I could do that. My nails dug into my palms as I tried to use the pain to stop me spiralling. Already, my thoughts flitted away from the meeting I was in, trying to trap me with worries; had I left the oven on? Had I fed Nibbles? What if I was fired?

"Elle!" Newton's voice cut through my spiralling thoughts.

"Y-yes," I squeaked. I counted the seconds until he spoke, using maths to anchor my brain.

"As I was saying, it is unusual for two graduates to work in the same area for their placements outside of Finance or one of the audit teams, but in this case, we feel that it would be prudent to allow it. You will learn a lot there and I believe it will be a suitable placement."

"So, I'm going to risk?" I couldn't believe it. This was exactly what I wanted. No one got what they wanted, did they? Especially not at the Bathory Corporation. My heart bounced up and I felt like I could soar. This was the best moment of my life.

"It is always up to you what you risk," Newton said. His lips twitched the tiniest amount. Was that a joke?

"And now the other news," Newton carried on.

My heart sank, plummeting like a yo-yo to hit the floor and spin there uselessly. *What other news?*

"About your powers."

"I don't have powers."

"Exactly."

I gaped between Newton and Ahmed. George didn't seem to know what was going on and twisted their head to take us all in.

Newton leaned forward, meeting my confused gaze. "You're a null."

Chapter 44

Nulls, also known as vacuums, voids or dims, are one of the most dangerous types of fae.

Ozark Bumblington – A History of Fae

George gasped.

My body felt light, as if I was having an out of body experience, except instead of floating up by the ceiling, I felt dragged down, plummeting below the earth. They thought I was useless, nothing, stupid. As I gulped for air, it was the last word that focused me.

I wasn't stupid. I wasn't nothing. My intelligence, in maths at least, was proven, quantifiable in my masters degree and my completed mensa maths puzzle books. Chanting quadratic equations in my head, I got some control over my trembling body.

I wasn't stupid.

And Ahmed had just given me a good report on my placement in the Archives, so, logically, null must mean something else.

"What's a null?" I asked, opening my notebook, and flipping to a new page. The fresh paper grounded me. Writing things down gave me something to do with my hands and made me feel more in control of whatever this situation was.

Newton nodded as if I'd passed some sort of test.

Ahmed shot my mentor a frustrated look. He probably had another speech lined up. The djinni coughed and started talking. "Nulls are a name given to a rare type of fae. They can come from any court and are hard to identify because of their ability to dull magic."

I paused in my notetaking and frowned. "You think I can stop magic?" That didn't make any sense.

"There are nuances. It is difficult to know because nulls are so rare. But, we know two things. One; they are the seventh child of a seventh child."

"Is that what's behind my lucky number?" I blurted out before pressing my lips together.

"I would not have thought so," said Newton. Of course not. That was just my crazy way of dealing with things. And now the mathematics genius knew I had a lucky number. I was an idiot.

Ahmed coughed. "And two; magic stops working around them, around you."

"That's ridiculous." I stopped, my eyes boggling out of my head. What was I thinking? This djinni was still my boss and I'd just said he was ridiculous.

Newton smiled. "Ah, it is about time somebody mentioned that awful waistcoat. Honestly, it is truly terrible, and I lived through a time of powdered wigs and arsenic face powder." Another joke?

Ahmed's eyes glowed a dangerous gold and power curled off him in tendrils of ruby glitter until he took a breath and calmed himself. "It is not ridiculous, Elle. It is a fine example of tailoring. And it is true, you are a rare fae." He leaned forward and gave me an encouraging smile. Unfortunately, the remnants of his power burst made it look more menacing, and I shrank back from him.

"But you've done magic around me lots of times." My notebook lay forgotten on my lap as I argued my point. If I'd had time to think, the irony would have been clear. I'd spent my entire life wishing I was special, wanting to have powers and praying that some supernatural would rescue me from whatever foster home I was living in, take me to their home and tell me I was really part of their world. Childish dreams. Now, Ahmed was telling me I was the opposite of special. I was a nothing, a null, a void, a nobody. And it was a good thing.

"Yes, I can perform magic, but I have not cast magic on you. And you broke through my wards." He raised a finger to emphasise his point as if that was the defining point.

George nodded along. "That makes sense."

"No, it doesn't. I didn't break through anything, and how do you know it was me? It might have been a fault in the spell."

Ahmed narrowed his eyes.

Newton's smile broadened, showing his pointed fangs. He was enjoying this.

My forehead creased. This was a mistake, maybe some sort of joke and I was missing the punchline.

"George, would you get me some papers from the desk?" Ahmed asked, his golden gaze never leaving me. "The second drawer on the right."

The minotaur obliged but couldn't open the drawer no matter how much they heaved.

"Elle, now you try."

I swallowed, but got up and stood next to George. They put one hand on my shoulder and gave me a reassuring squeeze. I reached out and tugged the drawer. There was no resistance, just a brief flicker of cobwebs over my skin that made me want to itch. It opened.

George beamed down at me as if I'd done an amazing party trick.

I stared back at Ahmed. A smug smile spread of the djinni's face.

"OK, so I opened a drawer. It's a drawer."

"It is a warded drawer. None but I should be able to open it. George, our strong minotaur friend, could not. But you," he wagged a finger at me, "you have broken through it like it was nothing. And this is not the first time."

"You value logic, Miss Bruma," Newton said, "as do I.

Please, consider the facts at hand."

My mind whirred. I had opened the drawer on my first day here, got into the restricted section and who knew what else. I was a null. I sank back into my chair. "How?"

"No one knows exactly, as I said, nulls are difficult to identify."

Newton leaned forward. "But what we do know is they are one of the most powerful supernaturals in existence."

Chapter 45

Magic in general will not work against a null fae.

Ozark Bumblington – *A History of Fae*

I shifted in my seat, uncomfortable with the three sets of eyes that pierced me. "What does that mean?" I grabbed my pen and notebook to centre myself, poised to make notes that I could dissect later on.

"It means that compulsions do not work on you, you can break through any wards and weaken any magic used against you. In short you would be perfect for any and all illegal activity that involves supernaturals."

Ahmed nodded along. "It is no wonder that the fae emperor has taken an interest in you."

"What?" Newton's outburst startled me. Fury raked across his features, revealing the monster inside the vampire.

I shrank back, a kitten hoping to avoid a lion by making

itself small and insignificant. I clutched onto the only thing that made sense. "I don't want to get involved in any illegal activity."

Newton shook his head and regained some of his composure although his eyes flashed a dangerous shade of red. "You may not have a choice. If others learn of this, they could kidnap you and try to use you."

"But you said compulsion doesn't work on me. I won't do it. I wouldn't."

Newton's eyes softened into something approaching sympathy. "There are other ways to force you to do what someone wants."

I inhaled a sharp breath. With all the talk of magic, I'd forgotten that there were simpler ways to get me to cooperate; instead of complex spells, someone could just torture me. I was weak, I'd give in. I scribbled myself a note to ask Precious for extra self-defence practice.

"And that is why we are the only people who know about this, and you are not to tell anyone about your abilities."

I nodded. Of course I wouldn't tell anyone. Why would I invite that sort of trouble into my life?

Newton returned my nod and adjusted his gold cufflinks. "I will have to let Elizabeth know, but we will keep this off your file and you will report to me if you notice anything suspicious. Agreed?"

I nodded again, struck mute by the speed my life got turned upside down.

"As far as anyone knows, you are a normal human, nothing special."

I stiffened my spine, sitting straighter in my chair. I might be a null, but I'd been a nothing my whole life and I'd clawed my way to where I was today through hard work and determination, and I wasn't going to let this label stop me from getting success. This time my nod was sharp.

Newton stood and strode across the carpeted floor to the lifts.

"Congratulations, Elle!" George stood, strode over and pulled me into another hug. This time I grinned, not even minding the physical contact. I was going to work in risk, with numbers and statistical probabilities and mathematical models. It would be glorious.

"Careful Mx Taurus, you don't want to be reported to HR. Good luck with your next placement, Miss Bruma." With that parting shot, Newton left, the elevator doors closing over him.

George dropped me like I was a hot potato. "Sorry, Elle. I didn't mean – it wasn't – sorry."

"Hey, it's OK." I patted George's arm. "I'm always happy to get a George hug."

"Pretty crazy, you being one of the most powerful supernaturals around."

"Nah, I'm just normal, remember?"

Chapter 46

Letting your emotions show is a sign of weakness.

Elizabeth Bathory - *The First Disrupter*

Working in risk management was all I'd ever wanted, so why didn't that help buoy my aching heart? It still pined for Liam. Stupid, traitor heart. I flung my Dating notebook across the room. I couldn't think about him. Today was the first day of my new placement and I'd spent enough time crying since I'd left him.

Combined with the renewed feelings of abandonment that had surged in me since I'd found our that my fae parents had dumped me in the foster system, possibly because they knew I was a null and I'd been a mess all weekend. Or maybe they were dead. I still didn't know. I had one piece of the puzzle but it only led to more questions.

I did the best I could with my makeup and chose my power suit, the one with shoulder pads to flesh out my skinny frame.

It was meant to lend me confidence, but when I looked in the mirror, all I saw was a pale, vulnerable girl playing dress up blinking back at me with huge red eyes, still raw from all the tears I'd shed. Abby said that crying was part of the healing process, but it sure looked like weakness and puffy eyes to me.

"Good luck today, and forget about him and your stupid parents. They're not worth it. They didn't get the joy of knowing you and they're the ones missing out, not you." Abby sent me off with a hug. I wished I could believe her words.

I forced myself to stride out of the door. I wasn't feeling confident, but I could fake it. I would fake it. Until I made it. A future director didn't break down because of personal drama, and they certainly didn't cry in the toilets.

I told myself that as I sobbed into a pile of tissues, locked in the ladies' loo.

This was not how I wanted my placement in risk to begin. I took some deep breaths, blew my nose again and forced myself out of the cubicle. I splashed some water onto my face and did my best to salvage my makeup. My face looked paler than usual, and my birthmark stood out against my cheek. Brilliant.

I undid my hair from its askew ponytail and redid it, stroking my fingers through my long hair until it gleamed purplish black in the bathroom lighting. My eyes looked red and puffy, but I didn't want to be late on my first day in the Risk

Management Community – they'd changed the company name of departments from Collective last week after an anonymous email got sent round with a Borg meme in it. Kylie had been furious. I had shared it with Abby and we'd shared a drink and a giggle about it in between my bouts of crying.

I stiffened my spine, looked my reflection in the eye and told myself that I would have a great first day.

With that, I headed to the risk management section of the second floor.

A tall lady with a severe bun greeted me and the other graduate starting his placement today. Clothilde Baumschon, Chief Risk Officer. I knew her face; I'd made a point of studying her company profile and any public interviews she'd given. The woman was amazing. Her acumen for figures and cutting through complex jargon was legendary. And if I could impress her, maybe I could be one of the Heads of Risk who strutted through the halls discussing standard deviations and loss parameters.

She looked us up and down, gave a small sniff and addressed us. "Welcome to risk management, the most important department in the banking arm of this company. We make day-to-day decisions about lending, managing interest rate risks, controls and operational risk as well as ensuring the company's compliance with ever changing regulations. Without the control that this department brings, the Bathory Corporation would not be able to lend as much or make as much profit. While you are in my domain, you will learn the secrets of optimal control and maximum value for risk investments. Do you have any questions?"

A hundred questions churned inside me, burning away the emotional pain that tore at my chest. I raised my hand level with my chin and, when Clothilde nodded in my direction, I sucked in a breath and asked, "What models do you find most effective for operational risk? Do you use generalised pareto distribution or do you find alternatives more useful?"

A small smile flicked over her tight lips, and she opened her mouth to answer me. Pride flooded through me. I was meant to be here.

The doors behind me slammed open with force. Clothilde's eyes widened a fraction before she became her composed self again. "Elizabeth. To what do we owe the pleasure of a CEO visit." There was an edge to Clothilde's voice, as if she were unhappy with the CEO waltzing into her department – sorry, collective – without notice.

"Clothilde. A pleasure as always. Your insights in yesterday's board meeting were as valuable as they always are."

Clothilde stiffened.

I stepped to one side to watch the exchange, keeping my features as neutral as possible while my two idols stood in front of me. Beside me, the other graduate boggled.

"Don't worry, I'm not here for you. I wanted," she clicked her fingers and Xavier, the executive assistant who dogged her steps, whispered a name, "Noelle Bruma."

"Me," I gasped and Elizabeth Bathory's dark gaze found me.

She walked over and gripped my chin, staring deep into my eyes. "Have you been crying?"

"Allergies," I muttered. I didn't want anyone to know my heart had been broken, much less by someone who worked here. I had probably broken some company rule just by going on a date with another employee. Adding 'check employee handbook' to my mental to do list, I met the CEO's gaze, wondering if she could see my roiling emotions in my eyes. Was that a power vampires had? And would it even work on me with my newfound abilities to resist magic? Something else to check.

Elizabeth studied me for another long moment before she released my chin. "Good. It wouldn't do for a member of my personal staff to cry at work."

"Your personal staff?" Clothilde raised an eyebrow. "I understood she was assigned to me for her next placement."

Elizabeth gave a dainty shrug. "Things change. After speaking with my executive advisor," that was Newton, "it seems she has a unique set of skills that will help with my campaign."

"I do?"

The CEO gave me a smile. "Don't sound so surprised. Ahmed has sung your praises to me, and we all know that you found the fraud in the fae account. I need someone with your...skills at my side."

My skills? She meant my newfound null abilities. "So I'm not going to spend my placement in risk management?" Disappointment tinged my voice.

"Don't worry about letting Clothilde down, she understands, don't you, Clotty?"

The Chief Risk Officer bared her teeth.

"You can have your pick of another graduate, if you like. Take it up with HR. I need this one with me." She placed a cold arm around my shoulders.

I repressed a shudder as she led me away from my dream department. But, this was good. I had come to the CEO's attention. I would work closely with her for the next few months, impress her and then I'd get my choice of permanent roles. This was a good thing. So why did I have to keep repeating it to myself?

"May I ask what campaign you need me on?" I managed to ask as Elizabeth Bathory swept me along to the lift that led to her private floor.

She stopped and tapped her foot as her executive assistant pushed the button for her. "Of course," she said with a grin that reminded me of a shark circling its prey, "I'm going to run for prime minister."

Epilogue

A bochdew typically takes the form of a rodent, but they are dangerous predators who are fiercely loyal to those they have bonded with.

Ozark Bumblington – *A History of Fae*

Nibbles munched on a sunflower seed, savouring its nutty taste and brittle texture when his fur prickled. A sure sign that his chosen was in danger.

Abandoning his seed, he climbed the bars of his cage until he got to the door. A quick flick of the push mechanism that kept it locked and a swift head butt and he was free. He stretched his back, feeling the joints click as he prepared himself to transform.

A shadowed shape loomed in the window.

Nibbles cocked his head. Something that could fly or climb. It didn't narrow down the type of attacker much. It wasn't an ooze; he was confident of that. Nibbles shrugged and wiggled his bottom, loosening the muscles in his back legs before he settled into a crouch, his dark eyes focusing on the intruder. He was ready.

A muffled click and the window slid open, and a humanoid figure slipped inside. It looked around. Nibbles licked his lips. Assassin or common thief, it didn't matter to him. No one threatened his chosen.

The figure moved in absolute silence to the bed where Elle slept, her breath coming in the regular beats of someone who has no idea of how much danger they were in. She wouldn't know. That was Nibbles' silent promise to her.

He had guarded her ever since she had found him wandering in the dirty streets after he'd been expelled from the fae realm, sent to find his chosen. Well, he'd found her. He'd no idea if she was who he had been meant to find, but she'd found him, and he'd snuggled up to her warm body and chosen her then and there.

When she'd wailed and shouted and sulked until the humans she lived with agreed he could stay, he knew he would do anything for her. He'd scrabbled for coins down the back of the sofa when the house was empty to help pay his way – money seemed to be important to these humans – but she hadn't ever complained about his cost. If his elaborate sleeping arrangements were anything to go by, she wanted to spend her cash on him.

He'd have been perfectly happy curled up on a blanket, but he had his cover to maintain. As a hamster. He'd flipped through one of the books on hamster care Elle had brought home once. His lip curled in disgust as he remembered the tiny dependent creatures. But the images had reinforced his idea of the shape he needed to be in. He'd been told to hide himself when he'd been thrown from the fae realm and so he had, using his innate magic to change forms and make himself smaller, more hamster-like, although he was still large for the species. more guinea pig sized, as his chosen's flatmate referred to him.

Nibbles flared his nostrils as the cloaked figure stepped towards his chosen, breathing in the crystal sharp scent of the fae realm. So the intruder was a fae. No matter. Nibbles shifted on his perch. He'd have one shot to make this a clean kill and not wake Elle.

Another step and the shadowy fae was in range. Nibbles leapt, shifting to his natural form as he did so.

The fae let out a muffled cry, more an expression of air than a shriek as Nibbles landed on their throat, winding the creature and shoving it to the ground. He cradled the fae as it fell, preventing it from making a noise that might wake his chosen.

Nibbles grinned at the fae, baring his many sharp teeth as they stared up at him in horror. Their hands scrabbled at his wiry fur, but couldn't hurt him thanks to his thick hide. Nibbles tightened his grip, squeezing any breath from the intruder before he lifted them above his head. He widened his mouth, dislocating his jaw and tilted his neck back. The fae squirmed in his grasp but he had them.

Nibbles breathed his toxic breath over the person who would harm his chosen and the fae fell still, unable to counter the poison that washed over them.

He lowered the fae into his throat and swallowed, downing them in three short gulps. Nibbles licked his lips and burped, heaving up part of the cloak onto the floor.

Elle stirred in her bed. Nibbles threw the cloak remnant into his cage – might as well not waste good nesting material – and shrank back to his hamster form.

A breeze rushed through the room, and his chosen shivered before waking. She sat up and brushed the sleep from her eyes, frowning at the open window.

She padded across the floor to close it and stopped when she saw Nibbles sitting in a patch of moonlight, licking his paws. "Nibbles? What are you doing out of your cage?"

~

Please leave a review, they help other readers find great books. And if you spotted any typos, let Gemma know at gemma@gemmaclatworthy.com

Want to know how Liam felt about their date? Scan the picture below for a bonus chapter!

Scan the picture below for a free prequel to the Vampire Graduate Scheme series and find out how Nibbles and Elle met.

Author's Note

I had a lot of fun researching medieval illustrated letters and marginalia for this book. The attention to detail in the medieval manuscripts is fascinating and, while I'm sure the subject matter made sense to them, I can only describe some of them as bizarre. If you haven't already seen any memes about these, it's worth a quick search online because some of the pictures are hilarious.

Thanks to my brother, Neil, for the maths fact about the circumference of a pint glass being longer than the height. I can confirm this holds true for standard pint glasses but suggest you're confident of the measurements before placing any bets on it!

And finally, while I was on a graduate scheme, I did not knowingly work for any vampires, and I survived without any shady fae dealings or putting any djinn lamps or staplers in jelly.

Thank you

A special thank you to my amazing patrons: Emma Ward, ZomBev, Mark Canty and Sueann Snow who always support me.

If you want to support Gemma, you can find her on www.patreon.com/G_Clatworthy for exclusive first reads of new stories.

You can also join her newsletter at www.gemmaclatworthy.com for free stories and follow Gemma on www.instagram.com/gemmaclatworthy, www.facebook.com/gemmaclatworthy or join the Facebook reader's group; Gemma's book wyrms.

Other Books by G Clatworthy

Vampire Graduate Scheme series:

Placement One: Fae Audits

Placement Two: The Archives

Placement Three: Executive Assistant

Books set in the same universe as Vampire Graduate Scheme:

Rise of the Dragons series:

Awakening

Solstice of Dragons

Equinox Betrayal

Darkest Deception

Attack on Avalon

Fated Bloodlines

Eat, Pray, Dragons

Magical Liaison Office (a short story collection)

Omensford series:

Bedsocks and Broomsticks

Cream Teas and Crystal Balls

Donkeys and Demons

Pumpkins and Popstars

Exes and Enchantments

Fae and Familiars

Gnomes and Necromancy

Children's Books

The Child Who series:

The Girl Who Lost Her Listening Ears

The Boy Who Lost His Listening Ears

The Girl Who Dreamed of Sleep

The Boy Who Dreamed of Sleep

Nanny Pastry series:

Nanny Pastry and the Nimble Ninjabread Man

Other books:

Coronavirus in the words of children

About the Author

Gemma started writing during the 2020 lockdown and loves fantasy fiction and dragons in particular. She lives in Wiltshire with her family and two cats and enjoys crafts of all kinds. You can read all her writing first on www.patreon.com/G_Clatworthy.

Or join the conversation at Gemma's book wyrms readers' group on Facebook.

She also writes children's books. You can find out more on her website www.gemmaclatworthy.com or follow her on Instagram (www.instagram.com/gemmaclatworthy) or Facebook (www.facebook.com/gemmaclatworthy).

www.gemmaclatworthy.com